THE ONE AND ONLY

Also by Francis King

FRANCIS KING

THE
ONE AND ONLY

Constable · London

First published in Great Britain 1994
by Constable and Company Ltd
3, The Lanchesters, 162 Fulham Palace Road
London W6 9ER
Copyright © Francis King 1994
The right of Francis King to be identified
as the author of this work has been asserted by
him in accordance with the Copyright, Designs
and Patents Act 1988
ISBN 0 09 473800 9
Set in Linotron Palatino 11 pt by
CentraCet Ltd, Cambridge
Printed in Great Britain by
St Edmundsbury Press Ltd
Bury St Edmunds, Suffolk

A CIP catalogue record for this book
is available from the British Library

FOR STANISŁAW

1

He could have written of my years in the Black Box. He could have written of the sunny years before that, and of the shadows that from time to time slanted across them, bringing a warping dampness. He could have written of our friendship; of Kensington and Como and Gladbury; of Dad, and Ma's lovers, and the particular lover, the one we called The One and Only. He could even have written about It, though I should have preferred him not to do so. But why did he have to reveal that it was Noreen, eleven years older than I (he specifies the precise difference), who prised open the lid of the Black Box and let me out; that we live seven miles from Brighton; that, as an antique dealer, I specialise in Staffordshire? Why did he have to give all those clues? Anyone with a pair of compasses can pinpoint our village; and anyone can look there for an antique shop with Staffordshire figures crowding the window. That he calls Noreen Nesta and that he calls me not by my former name and not by my present name but (why choose something so weird?) by the fictitious name Otto Cramp, is not going to put anyone persistent off the scent.

When I write 'anyone persistent', I mean, of course, any journalist. I have begun to feel like one of those war criminals who, after decades of hard-working and respectable obscurity, suddenly find themselves blinking in terror in the arc-light of publicity.

He's a distinguished scientist, a Nobel Prize winner; and of course any distinguished scientist has the right to write his own life. But does he have the right to write mine too? I can hear his answer: 'If you wished to photograph a rambler rose and the rose was intertwined with another rose, then you would have to photograph both roses, wouldn't you?' But does an autobiography have to have the accuracy of a snapshot? Can't the photograph be a studio one, tactfully airbrushed here and there?

I put down the typescript on the sofa. Then, in case Noreen or Mrs P. should pick it up (like most women, they are as inquisitive as sniffer dogs) I stuff it into the bottom drawer of my desk under the used cheque books, the bank statements, the dividend vouchers.

It is time that I carried Noreen's breakfast up to her.

'Well, how are you, old dear?'

'Not so much of the old!' Noreen is now eighty-three. She no longer plays tennis, accompanies me on my long walks on the downs, or runs up the stairs to this bedroom, as she used to do a year ago. But she still hobbles out, leaning on the blackthorn stick which belonged to her father, to post a letter at the post box at the first corner of our street or to arrange the flowers in St Cuthbert's at the second.

I set down the tray on her kneehole desk and pull back the curtains. Then I fetch the bed-rest. I do all these things with love and gratitude. 'You've married your mother,' Bob told me years ago, before we had stopped seeing each other. But I never felt such love or such gratitude for poor old Ma.

[8]

'So how are we feeling this morning?'

With others she is courageously dismissive of her illness, but never with me. 'Oh, I had a ghastly night. I hardly slept a wink.'

I do not tell her that through the early hours I lay awake in the room next door, listening to her snoring. Instead I put an arm round her: 'Poor darling! Why don't you have the morning in bed?'

'I wouldn't dream of such a thing!' She raises a hand, knobbly with the arthritis which has made an invalid of her, up to my cheek and strokes it. 'I want to finish that picture for Ellen's birthday.' She no longer paints as she used to do when she rescued me from the Black Box; but she makes these collages out of dried leaves and flowers, which I must now collect for her, since she is no longer strong enough to collect them for herself. I take the hand in mine, turn it over, and kiss the palm.

'Has the post arrived?'

'Oh, it arrived ages ago,' I say without thinking. 'It's that new postman – far better than old Harry.'

'Anything interesting?'

If I were truthful, I should answer: 'Only something which may destroy our lives.' But I shake my head. 'Nothing. Some circulars, that's all. What they call junk mail.' Then to change the subject, I ask her: 'Would you like me to butter that toast?' On a good day she can manage the task; but I have a feeling that today may be a bad one.

'Would you, dear? Thank you.'

After I have left her, I have almost an hour before I open the shop.

Instead of reading *The Times*, as I usually do, I go to the drawer and take out the typescript. Once again I read that chapter about our school-days, this time slowly, not racing through it with a palpitating heart, as on the first occasion after I had looked in the index, still without page numbers, and seen all those entries under not my own name, Mervyn Frost, and not under my present name, Maurice Yates, but under that absurd name Otto Cramp. I should never have realised that Otto Cramp was I, were it not for that first entry, 'first meeting at Gladbury', and that second entry, 'holiday with mother of', and all those subsequent entries, at least a dozen of them.

This will kill Noreen, I think in fury and despair; and then I think: This will kill me. I am like a fox gone to earth; and now, because of this book, I can hear the panting of the hounds. Somehow I must destroy the book. But how can I do that? And why did he send it to me, still only in typescript, with no covering letter of explanation or excuse? Long ago, I finished with him and I thought that he had finished with me.

Noreen is calling. I shout up the stairs. 'Yes? What is it?'

'Sorry, darling. I wonder if you . . . The blasted paper has fallen off the bed.'

I run up the stairs and pick up the *Guardian* for her.

'There you are, old thing.'

'I told you not so much of the old!'

She is laughing that ageless laugh of hers.

My first customer is a middle-aged woman in a black velvet beret pulled over one ear. Her insteps bulge over court shoes which seem uncomfortably small for her feet, and her midriff bulges over a skirt which seems uncomfortably tight for her stomach. She has a sunnily optimistic expression on her face, as she begins to unwrap the parcel which she has been carrying under her arm.

'I've got to sell this,' she explains, without revealing what 'this' is. 'The usual problem. My old man's been made redundant after seventeen years with the same firm. I ask you!' She drops the brown paper on to my desk. 'There! It's been in the family for yonks. Dante Gabriel Rossetti. It's only a drawing, I know. But it ought to be worth quite a lot. I wonder if you'd be interested. Would you?'

I peer at the drawing, a head and shoulders of Elizabeth Siddal. Then I realise that it is one that I have seen in the V & A. I sigh my regret. 'I'm afraid – I'm terribly afraid . . . It's not an original drawing, you see, it's a print.'

Chin pulled in, she draws herself up, affronted. 'Oh, I don't think you can be right about that. I'm sure you can't. It was given to my in-laws as a wedding present years and years ago. By some rich relative. When we got married, they passed it on to us.'

'I'm terribly sorry.'

She begins to rewrap the picture, with angry, flustered movements. 'Perhaps I should take it up to Sotheby's. Or Christie's. Let an expert see to it.'

'Yes, you could certainly do that. But I think you'll find you'll be told the same thing.'

'Well, thank you for your trouble.' She gives her head a toss and then puts a hand up to straighten the beret.

'Thank you.'

Even before she has shut the door of the shop decisively behind her, I succumb to the pathos of the incident. For a moment it distracts me from the devouring pain, as of a duodenal ulcer, occasioned by that book. Then the pain returns. What is to happen? What am I to do?

I lower myself into the bergère chair which Colonel

Sprott has been dithering whether to buy for most of this summer, and begin to think of the Black Box, hemmed in by its dripping privet, of the months of silence, and of my deliverance by Noreen.

2

Len was one of the Guardians (that was what, male or female, I used to call them, giving them a capital letter in my mind). He was young and, since his lard-coloured body was huge, one might have supposed that during those years of War he would have been in the forces. But he had what he called 'my condition', necessitating that he inject himself each day with insulin. Once, entering what I thought was the deserted assembly room, I found him lying on his side, his buttocks and legs on the dais and his head and torso on the floor below it. I concluded with satisfaction: Well, he's dead, and left him there, for someone else to find. Someone else, his wife, who worked in the kitchens, did find him; but he wasn't dead, he was merely in a coma.

Len would lean over my armchair or he would squat beside it. 'How are we, Merv?' No one else had ever called me anything other than Mervyn. 'How are we today then? Aren't we going to say something? Come on, Merv! Speak to me! Say something! I'm your pal!' But I never said anything to anyone. That silence of mine tantalised him and even drove him to frenzy. He was like a small child with a jar of sweets or a money box that he was unable to open. Once, enraged, he slapped me across the back of my head, the small child hurling the jar or money box to the floor. 'You bloody well answer when you're spoken to!' he shouted at me. I merely blinked at him, my eyes watering from the violent blow. Then he put a hand, tattooed with a swallow (could it be that he had once done bird?), on to the back of my neck and gently stroked it. 'Sorry about that, Merv. But you can be terribly irritating, you know. A real pain.'

All day, except when summoned to meals, I used to sit in that armchair and stare at the garden. Because of a wartime shortage of staff, it was overgrown, a few rose-beds excepted. Was it always overcast or raining or did I, because of my illness, imagine that? I can still see the laurels glistening. I can still even hear the rain-drops lisping off them. Perhaps my illness, which the psychiatrists constantly argued about, induced in me a hyperaesthesia. How otherwise could I have heard those drops when I was separated from them by thick panes of glass?

I had seen Noreen on a number of occasions, but without any interest. I did not then know that she had been released from the ATS (she had been working in camouflage) because her mother was dead and her elderly father was dying; or that, twice each week, she gave art classes which any of the inmates could attend. No doubt Dr Unwin or Dr Lazarides had mentioned the classes to me, suggesting that they might be of benefit to me. No doubt Len had urged me: 'Why don't you

[13]

attend one of these art classes, Merv? Could give you an interest.' But those were days when I took nothing in.

Noreen was larger and more upright than she is now. Thirty-three years old, she had the ruddy complexion and the sturdy physique of the farm girl that once she had been. Her hands were big and capable, and she wore her thick, straight blonde hair parted in the middle and caught up at each side by a tortoiseshell clasp shaped like a butterfly. She had been at the Slade and had had a single picture, of harvesting on the farm below a thunderous sky, accepted by the Academy in 1938. Whenever she hurried through the living-room to the art room beyond it, she would look over to me, as I sat in 'my' armchair (by now, every other inmate knew that it was mine and made no effort to usurp it), staring out of the window. But I would pretend to be totally unaware of her. In fact, for most of the time I was totally unaware of her.

Then, one day, instead of clattering in her lumpy, flat-heeled shoes straight over the worn linoleum to the door to the art room, she veered towards me. 'Come on!' she said briskly. 'Join us! You don't want to sit there mooning day after day.'

I made no answer. I continued to stare out of the window.

'Oh come on!'

Many people had said, in effect, 'Come on!' to me, and I had ignored all of them. Why did I not ignore her? Was it some prescience, a leap of the mind into the future in place of its constant dawdling in the past, so that I knew, knew at once, that here was my rescuer and that, if I seized my opportunity, somehow, at some time, I should escape from the Black Box?

That first day she gave me some glitterwax to model,

[14]

and from it I made for her – yes, it was for her, not for myself – a rose with stiff pink and white petals, smelling vaguely of paraffin. 'Well done!' she told me. 'I think you've got a talent. A real talent.' I had heard her say the same thing or something like it to many of the other people also at work. But nonetheless I was delighted.

Every Tuesday and every Friday morning I used to wake in a state of expectation and happiness. She was coming, there would be a class. I still did not speak, to her or to anyone else. But when I saw her, I would give her a smile, such as I gave to no one else. 'You have the most wonderful smile in the world,' she was later to tell me. When she once opened her desk while I was standing by it, I noticed, with rare pleasure, that there, among the crayons and tubes of paint and scraps of paper, was my glitterwax rose.

When I at last spoke, I surprised myself as much as her.

All that week snow had been falling, smothering the laurels and lying thick on the garden paths. In the art room she wore her tweed overcoat and the tip of her nose was blue. In those days I myself was impervious to both cold and heat. I was never aware of the temperature, often prompting Len to fuss over me – I should put on a pullover, it was perishing; or why didn't I take my jacket off, I'd be boiled to death?

Noreen came over to me at the work table where I was moulding another lump of glitterwax. 'I think you've progressed beyond that,' she said. 'Why don't you try some painting? It could be more fun. It'll stretch you more. Yes?'

'Yes.'

It was only a monosyllable. But it was, literally, the first word which I had spoken since I had entered the

Black Box. Had she realised that? I asked her much later, for her to answer that yes, she had realised it, and then to add, in a puzzled tone: 'And, you know, I knew, I just knew as soon as I'd put the question, that, after so often refusing to answer me, you were going to answer me then.'

Yes.

It was a Yes to her, to myself, above all to life.

That was when she first fitted the key into the lock on the Black Box. The opening of the lid would come much later, long after the War was over. But that was when my deliverance was first put in train.

3

Noreen's head, an ancient Jaqmar scarf covering it (she often used to wear the scarf when bicycling over from the farm to the Black Box), appears round the door. 'No customers?'

'Only one. And she wasn't here to buy but to sell.' I tell her about the affronted woman with the print which she believes to be an original drawing.

Noreen sighs at the end of the story. 'This recession!' she says. It is fortunate that, because of the money left to her by her father, we have never had to live on the proceeds of the shop. 'I'm just going to toddle up the road to the post.'

'Oh, leave it to me! I'll take the letters later.'

'No, no, it's good for me to make the effort. I mustn't become housebound like poor old Mrs Green.'

She moves over to the door. Then she pauses, turns back. Her hand is on my head, the fingers running through my hair in a way that vaguely irritates me (later I shall have to jerk a comb through it), although I never tell her so.

'Is everything all right?'

'Yes, of course. Why?'

'You seem . . . Oh, I don't know.'

'Well, I am a little worried. Business couldn't be worse.'

'I'm afraid this is a period when most things couldn't be worse.'

I know that she knows that I am lying. She always does.

'Ah, well!' She sighs and moves away again.

Turning my head so that I can look out of the window and up the streets, I watch her as she hobbles along, her body almost a hairpin over the blackthorn stick. I admire her gallantry, as I have always admired it. As once over those three stillborn children (she was far too old for maternity, Dr Lewes tactlessly told her), so now over the crippling and agonising arthritis she never complains except to me. 'With you I can always let my hair down,' she often says.

Once again I begin to think of that typescript.

4

'I've never believed in miracles but in your case . . .' Dr Unwin had a blackhead on the side of his bulbous nose. I yearned to tell him to squeeze it. Having long ago discovered that he and I had both been to Gladbury – he, of course, long before me – he would often waylay me to talk about the school. When Bob, now at Oxford in the immediate aftermath of the War, came to see me, Dr Unwin would also talk to him about it. What had happened to old so-and-so? Was it true that old so-and-so had gone for a Burton over Germany? Bob, surprisingly, almost always knew the answers.

Dr Unwin made a steeple of his podgy fingers. 'I'm going to recommend your release,' he told me. 'I don't see the remotest possibility of any further problems. Dr Lazarides is not quite as, er, sanguine as I am, but then' – his body shook with the mirth which eventually erupted as a gulping laugh – 'he's always been a terrible pessimist. He once tried to convince me that we were on a losing wicket in the War.'

Standing at my shoulder, as I sat at the easel – it was summer, we were all out in the garden – Noreen asked me: 'So where will you go?'

I shrugged. 'Search me!'

'You could come to the farm.' It was as simple as that.

*

[18]

'You're crazy!' Bob protested when I told him the plan. 'She'll get her hooks into you. Mark my words!'

'Oh, I don't mind if she does.'

'She'll marry you before you know what's happened.'

'And I don't mind if she does that either.'

My insouciance infuriated him. 'She's over the hill, for God's sake! She's old enough to be your mother!'

Two – or was it three? – times he came out to the farm. Noreen was charming to him, but he would hardly speak to her. All his talk was of the old days – do-you-remember talk, as Noreen called it. Then he stopped coming. The next Christmas there was a card, addressed to me alone, and a few months after that a wedding invitation – he was marrying a young French widow with a title – also addressed to me alone. For a few more years – by now he was in the States – we wrote to each other. Then silence . . .

Until that typescript arrived.

5

Of course I had seen Bob before; but it was only at the Novices Boxing Competition, in which all the thirteen- and fourteen-year-old new boys had to take part, that I was drawn to him.

Sarge, who had been first an Army PT champion and then an Army PT instructor, was in charge. Small and sturdy, with grotesquely over-developed calf, arm and shoulder muscles and a square head on which the greying hair was cropped short, he had lost part of his left forefinger when, so he maintained, a monkey had bitten it off during service in India. When Bob first heard this, in the gym, he hissed at me: 'What do you suppose he was doing to the monkey?'

I had learned to box at my preparatory school because Dad, who had once been middle-weight champion at Gladbury, had wanted me to learn and I was eager to please him. I was never much good at it; but at least, when my turn came to enter the ring at Sarge's summons, I was able to hold my own against the thin, pallid boy, at least six inches taller than I, who was my opponent. As though by tacit agreement, he made no attempt to punch me hard and I made no attempt to punch him hard.

Bob, so tiny, and his opponent, so hefty, had been matched with what I could only assume was deliberate cruelty by Sarge. The curious thing about Bob was the spherical size of his head – 'Bighead' eventually became his nickname – in comparison with the tadpole size of a body which dwindled away into the shortest of legs and the smallest of feet. Repeatedly his opponent punched out at that head, with a viciousness of which Sarge and the older spectators all too clearly approved. Bob could do little but raise his gloved fists now to his mouth and now to his nose, in a vain attempt to shield them. Each time that he rocked back on his heels, there was a gasp of delight from everyone present, with the exception of myself. When some blood began to trickle out of one of his nostrils, one or two people even cheered. Never good at blood, I was beginning to feel vaguely sick and faint. Why the hell didn't Sarge stop the fight?

At the end of the third round – there were five in all

– Sarge did in fact ask Bob: 'Is that enough for you?' But, unable to speak, Bob vigorously shook his head, at the same time curling up a tongue to lick at the blood now trickling down the cleft below his nose.

'Very well,' Sarge barked. 'Proceed!'

I felt an extraordinary pity for this wretched little creature being pounded by someone so much stronger and larger; but I also felt an extraordinary admiration. By not giving in, by shaking his head instead of nodding it, as I would certainly have done, at Sarge's question, he had, in a strange way, simultaneously got the better of Sarge, responsible for this cruel mismatching, of his triumphant opponent and of the gloating spectators. Later I was to feel a similar combination of pity and admiration when he submitted, without any sound, without any indication of fear before or pain after, to ferocious beatings from the monitors. That he showed neither of those emotions of course only made them the more energetic in their punishment of him. I myself went through my school-days without ever being beaten more than once in the course of a term. Bob, repeatedly leaving the light on in the study when he was the last to quit it, failing to clean his shoes, omitting to take a cold shower, was beaten at least once each week.

A hand pressed to his still-bleeding nose, Bob came and sat down beside me at the ringside. After my own bout I had at once rushed off to shower and change, and now wondered why he did not do likewise. I looked surreptitiously at him, noticing that there was even blood smeared on one of his shoulders, that there was a hole in one of his gym shoes, through which I could glimpse the tip of a grubby big toe, and that his thick, blond hair looked as if it had received a basin cut. I drew a handkerchief out of my pocket and handed it

[21]

to him. Without a word, he took it from me and pressed it to his nose. When he handed it back, he said: 'Soak it in cold water. That way it won't stain.'

So began our friendship.

He was far cleverer than I, confiding in me that, but for a scholarship, his missionary parents in India would never have been able to send him to Gladbury. Having won the scholarship, he had disconcerted and displeased everyone by announcing that he wished to study not Classics – Gladbury was famous for its Classical side – but what was then generally known as 'stinks'. Attempts were made to dissuade him; but his was a granite obstinacy.

'I wonder why we've become friends,' he mused to me on one occasion during that first term, when on a bicycle ride through the lush summer countryside, we had stopped for tea at a farmhouse. 'We've nothing in common.' He thought for a while, savagely chewing, as he so often did to my disgust, at the stump of a finger-nail. Then he said: 'Perhaps that's why we are friends. The attraction of opposites.'

I constantly marvelled at the contrast between Bob's mental agility and his physical clumsiness. At the horse in the gym, Sarge would stand in his dazzlingly white gym shoes, his beautifully pressed white flannels, his immaculately laundered white singlet. As each of us arrived at the run to leap-frog over it, he would bark a falsetto 'Hup!', extending a hand in case any of us fell. Bob would lope, not run, up to the horse, on his face a self-deprecating grin which only intensified Sarge's contempt and hatred for him. 'Hup!' But instead of accelerating, he would diminish his pace, until he was walking as he neared Sarge. Then he would begin to clamber over the horse.

'Williams, you're a disgrace, you're an utter disgrace. Are you a girl or something?'

Bob grinned. 'I don't think so, sir. Maybe you'd like to have a look to make sure.' That was one of the many occasions on which he was beaten for 'cheek'.

6

Noreen has returned. First I hear her stick on the pavement, then I see her humped back.

'You've taken a long time,' I say.

Noreen explains that she ran into one of our neighbours, the widow of a general, who shares her interest in antique dolls. The neighbour has just bought a Schoenhut doll, which is equipped not only with a combination of steel springs and swivels to enable all its limbs to be moved but also with an elaborate apparatus to enable it to stand upright. 'I'd just love to have it.' She herself possesses a large collection of dolls, which she refuses to let me sell, however much we are offered for them by would-be purchasers like the general's widow. Can these dolls, I often wonder, be a surrogate for the children she so much wanted but could never bear? I myself never wanted children, much less dolls.

'With luck I'll get you that German bisque doll at Bonhams tomorrow.'

'Oh, that'll fetch a fortune! Kammer and Reinhart dolls always do.'

'Wait and see.'

I am determined that, whatever the cost, I will buy her the doll.

7

Years later, when I was no longer Mervyn Frost but Maurice Yates, I was confronted by Sarge, long since retired from Gladbury.

Noreen's father had died, after a long and savage illness, and for a while we had attempted to run the farm ourselves. But Noreen really wanted only to paint and I, a recluse, terrified that my true identity would be discovered, was totally without any aptitude for the life of a gentleman farmer. There had been a bitter conflict between father and daughter when she had announced that she would marry me; but eventually he had come to accept me, not because of my love for her but because of my love for the antiques with which the rambling farmhouse, part Jacobean, part Queen Anne, part Victorian, was crammed. He, too, loved these pieces – not, like me, for their beauty, but because of what they represented in the long history of his family. It pleased him when I would spend hours on end repairing a Sheraton-style beech chair with a tattered cane-work back, found in the attic, or carefully polished the tambour shutter of a writing-table stuffed almost to bursting point with old receipted bills. From the

Brighton public library, to which I never ventured, Noreen would bring me back books on antiques; but I learned more from the emaciated old boy, his voice faintly droning on about how that fold-over pedestal rosewood table had been inherited from his Aunt Flora, and how that porter's chair in panelled mahogany over there had been bought for a song, an absolute song, at an auction sale up at the Old Rectory in the middle of the War.

It was natural therefore that, when the old man had died – Noreen found him lying out by the pond in the garden, his elderly golden retriever seated beside him, as though patiently waiting for him to wake up and get on with the painfully slow walk on which he was taking her – and when we had at last succeeded in selling the house and the farm to a Canadian businessman who had made his fortune in scrap during the War, we should decide to move to London. What place was more likely to assure my anonymity?

At first we stayed in a Bayswater hotel, from the bedroom window of which I could look out on the Park. As the winter evening closed in prematurely, I could also look out on the prostitutes who, at that period, would wait along the railings, in serried rank as though on guard, for their randy, shifty customers. Once, catching me there, Noreen asked me 'Tempted?' 'No, only curious.' That was the truth. I was fascinated by the furtive and perilous lives of those shadowy women out there in the cold; but I had no wish to go out and speak to any of them, much less to accompany any of them back to her room. I never wanted anyone but Noreen.

Noreen was now teaching art at a small private girls' school, as well as painting those pictures, with their cramped brush-work and over-attention to detail,

[25]

which in later years would, like the prostitutes before them, line the railing separating Bayswater Road from the Park to tempt reluctant buyers. I would spend most of the day in our high-ceilinged double bedroom, reading about antiques or the history of crime. Of the crime, perhaps with good reason, Noreen disapproved – wasn't it a little morbid (she repeatedly used that word) to be interested in it? Sometimes, restlessness suddenly blowing through me like a breeze unexpectedly shifting the sluggish air of a thunderous afternoon, I would wander out, to mooch along the Portobello Road or Kensington Church Street, staring in at the windows of antique shops and junk shops. Occasionally I would buy something small, a brooch or a necklace for Noreen, some cuff-links for myself, a single Vincennes cup and saucer, a Venetian glass tazza, a baccarat-spaced millefiori. 'Where are you going to put that?' Noreen would ask. The answer was in a drawer, or at the bottom of the wardrobe, or in one of the suitcases gathering dust on top of the wardrobe, or under our double bed.

After some months, we decided to look for a flat, largely because there was no room left for these sporadic acquisitions. We could certainly afford one; and in a flat there would be adequate space not merely for the antiques but for Noreen's painting.

Our flat-hunting took us to a vast Edwardian block, its ornate façade presenting a liver-coloured, much-pitted cliff to a dark, narrow street off Westbourne Grove. Craning our necks upwards to its small, blind windows, we both knew at once that we could never bear to live there. But none the less we entered. The hall was shabby but clean. The house agents had told us to make contact with the porter and so, after some hesitation, we descended to the basement. After we had rung at the bell with 'Porter' inscribed in its highly polished brass, there was a long pause. Then a small, elderly, stiffly upright man, with a coxcomb of white hair sticking straight up from above his forehead, opened the door. His face had the congested look of the hard drinker, his breath smelled of whisky. 'Yes?'

With terror I recognised him as Sarge. The left forefinger, with its missing top joint, was unmistakable. Would he recognise me, despite my moustache and beard, despite the way in which my hair was now parted not at the side but in the middle, despite my paunch and my premature wrinkles and stoop?

We explained why we had come, and Sarge, who was wearing an open-necked shirt and baggy flannels, then said crossly: 'One moment, please' and shut the door on us. Eventually he reappeared, now in a fawn uniform, with a black tie. 'Sorry,' he said, jangling some keys.

The flat was desolate, its narrow corridors doubling through a labyrinth of small, damp rooms. Noreen was fascinated by an ancient refrigerator, a yellowing funnel sticking out of its top and its door ajar on its rusty interior – 'My Sanders grandmother had one just like that. It used to remind me of a ship.'

'Of course it needs a lot of doing over,' Sarge said dolefully. 'The old couple lived here for nigh on fifty years. Then they went and died within a week of each other. Lucky for them! Neither could have managed alone.'

There were relics of the old couple everywhere: scattered copies of *Reader's Digest* on the hearth of a bedroom; a butcher's apron, hanging behind a door; a

[27]

wardrobe which tottered and all but fell on top of Noreen when, out of perverse curiosity, she tugged to open it.

'I have a feeling this isn't the one for you,' Sarge eventually said, in a voice which implied: 'Why the hell are you wasting my time?'

Noreen sighed. 'There's something about it . . . the atmosphere . . .'

'That's what they all say. But redecoration would soon make the atmosphere okay. It usually does.'

Perhaps he was right. Perhaps we could have made something of it. The price was cheap enough. But eventually Noreen said: 'There's no point in wasting any more of our time,' and Sarge answered sourly: 'Or in wasting mine.'

I had a ten-shilling note (worth a good sum in those days) ready to tip him. In the hall I drew it out of my trouser pocket and held it out. 'Thank you for your trouble,' I said.

Suddenly Sarge was squinting at me, his mouth open under the small, bristly white moustache. 'You know . . . I have the strangest feeling . . . I've met you before. Wasn't you – wasn't you at Gladbury?'

'Gladbury? The school, you mean?' Could he apprehend my terror, behind my attempted nonchalance? 'No, as a matter of fact, I was at Harrow.'

Again he squinted at me. Then his face neared mine, I could smell his whisky-laden breath. He looked malevolent, accusatory. 'I could have sworn . . . You remind me so much . . .'

Noreen hastened to the front door and I strolled after her (don't hurry, don't hurry). I turned: 'I'm sorry to have troubled you for nothing. Thank you so much.'

'The chap you remind me of – it's an interesting story . . . Maybe you read about it in the papers at the time.'

[28]

But Noreen had pushed the swing door open and gone through it. Hurrying now, I followed her.

8

During our second year at Gladbury Bob's father, on leave from India, came to lecture one Sunday. I was astonished by how old he looked, with a wispy white beard and a fringe of white hair around his otherwise bald, bulging cranium. He wore a crumpled linen jacket and black trousers, exposing his black, woollen socks, and a soiled dog-collar. Bob's mother was with him, and she too looked far too old to have a son so young, and far too virginal, with her pale, narrow face, and pale, thin lips, to have a son at all.

The lecture was about the work of the mission in southern India, and Bob was deputed by his father to operate the lantern. There was a lot of giggling when the slides appeared upside down or when, Mr Williams having clicked repeatedly with the small device in his right hand, they appeared not at all. 'Oh, come on, Bob!' he would exclaim irritably; or 'Oh, for heaven's sake! Wake up!'

There were fuzzy pictures of colleagues, some white but most brown, who were doing 'an absolutely marvellous job', who were 'quite selfless', who were 'totally indispensable'. We were shown sufferers from leprosy, grinning abjectly into the camera while they displayed a bandaged hand or foot; a deformed baby without any arms; a man whose right leg had swollen to a huge size because of elephantiasis. Later Bob told me that, while

[29]

he was still with his parents in India, he had seen an elephantiasis sufferer whose 'balls reached amost to the floor – bigger than footballs'. Mr Williams spoke of how the love of God reconciled all these people to the sadness of their fates. He also spoke repeatedly of the need for funds, no doubt because after the lecture there was to be a collection.

The headmaster, Mr Curry, sat up on the dais beside the screen, glowering at us each time that a mishap with the slides caused us to giggle. Perhaps I giggled more loudly than the others. Certainly I was all at once aware that it was at me personally that he was now glowering, rather than at the whole assembly. I bit the inside of my cheek, I pretended to blow my nose violently.

'I want you to give really generously,' Mr Curry exhorted us when the lecture was over. 'I'm sure you all agree that this is a cause deserving of all the support that we can offer.'

Later Bob told me that he had put a button into the bag when it was passed to him, before its descent among the rest of us. So it was that, when on the following Sunday Mr Curry came to announce the total, he told the congregation that he was glad that the sum was as large as sixteen pounds, three shillings, two pence and – a *button*. There was contempt in the emphasis which he gave to the last word.

Mr Williams thanked us all for having been such an attentive audience. He seemed to have been totally unaware of our giggles. We clapped hesitantly, unsure whether this was appropriate on a quasi-religious occasion. He gave a little bow and grinned, to reveal ill-fitting butter-yellow false teeth. Then he turned to Bob: 'All right, Bob. Just bring the slides with you and I'll see to the projector.'

Bob pushed the last two slides into the second of the two boxes, each made of battered leather, and then got to his feet, one box in either hand. He approached the edge of the dais on which the projector had been placed and stared at me. I knew that reckless, impudent look so well. Then he stepped off the dais. With an 'Oops!', he slipped, foundered, crashed to the floor. The boxes bounced on either side of him, with a sound of shattering glass. I was certain that he had skilfully engineered the apparent accident.

'Oh, you – you stupid, stupid boy! You nincompoop! Can't you ever do anything right?' Mr Williams was livid. Then he controlled himself: 'Oh, never mind, never mind! Let's see the extent of the damage.' He hurried across the hall, from one dais to the other, and opened one of the boxes. Shards of glass scattered from it. Then he wailed: 'Oh, lord, lord, now what am I going to do? The day after tomorrow I'm supposed to be giving this talk at Sedbergh and on the day after that . . . It'll be no good without slides.'

The boys tried to humiliate 'Bighead' about his parents. 'They're ancient!' one of the monitors told him. 'Are you sure that they're not your grandparents?' someone took up, and another: 'Or your great-grandparents?'

'How on earth did they manage to do it?' The question, from a boy with the features of a fox, evoked general guffaws.

Bob smiled, totally unfazed. 'Well, you've heard of Isaac in the Bible, haven't you? His father Abraham was a hundred years old when he was born and his mother was ninety. My father and mother are a modern Abraham and Sarah. That's all.' He shrugged his shoulders, pulled a face and laughed. As so often, he

[31]

had cleverly undercut their ridicule. There was nothing worse that anyone could say.

9

One Parents' Weekend during that second year, when Ma was away in Monte Carlo with the rich, elderly man whom both she and I called The Lord of Hosts, because he was a peer and because he gave such frequent and lavish parties, Bob suggested that I should have lunch with him and his parents in the hotel at which they were staying. Ma always stayed at the four-star Dolphin, even though on one occasion there had been a fuss about a cheque which had bounced, not once but twice; but the Williamses had put up at what was more a pub than a hotel, surrounded by housing estates far out in the sprawling, smoky suburbs. To reach it, Bob and I had to use our bicycles.

As we sat down in the dining-room, I was already wishing that I had not agreed to come. Another boy, whose father owned a Lagonda and whose mother had been on the stage, had also invited me to lunch. I did not much like the boy, but to be with them all on a picnic near Tintern Abbey or on the banks of the Wye now seemed far preferable.

'Shall we all have the soup?' Mrs Williams said firmly, after a perusal of the menu. Ma had often told me that 'No one who is anyone has soup at luncheon.' But I nodded: 'Fine.' 'And the roast pork afterwards?' I nodded again. 'Oh, and some ginger beer for the boys,'

[32]

she told the waitress. 'You'd like ginger beer, boys, wouldn't you?'

'Frost would much rather have some real beer,' Bob said. 'That's what he always drinks when he's out with his mother.'

Both parents stared at me in shocked amazement.

'No, no. He's talking nonsense. Please!' I had begun to blush. 'Ginger beer is fine.'

'Oh, do stop playing the ass!' Bob's father told him.

Literally playing the ass, Bob hee-hawed, making everyone in the dining-room turn round.

'Bob! Stop that!' His mother slapped the menu down on to the table top. She looked yellow and tired. Later, Bob was to tell me that she suffered from recurrent bouts of malaria.

'Sorry, Mater, sorry!' I doubt if he had ever called her 'Mater' before.

Mr Williams, clearly feeling obliged to make conversation with me but at a loss how to do so, began to question me about my studies. How far had I progressed in Latin? What period of history were we doing in my class? Was I past quadratic equations? He even ventured a question in French, in a terrible accent, to test how proficient I was in the language. Through all this inquisition I could not help noticing how much food he and his wife devoured. 'Isn't either of you interested in any more of these excellent roast potatoes?' he asked at one moment; and at another moment it was she who was asking: 'No one for any more parsnips? We don't want to waste them, do we?'

We sat in the lounge over coffee so weak that it might have been tea. Bob had found, among a pile of out-of-date copies of *Punch*, *Farmer's Weekly*, *The Lady* and

Tatler, one of those puzzles once so common in the waiting-rooms of dentists. Face screwed up with determination, he lay back in his chair, tipping the little balls now this way and now that.

Eventually his mother said: 'Oh, Bob, do put that down and drink your coffee!'

For a moment he did put it down. Then, having sipped at his coffee, he picked it up again.

'Oh, for heaven's sake, Bob!' Now it was his father.

Even then, I had a strong social sense. I was as bored as Bob but I would never have dreamed of revealing that I was. Desperately I tried to make conversation, now putting my own questions to Mr Williams instead of answering his. Was it terribly hot during the summer in India? Had he ever shot a tiger? ('Oh, dear me, no! What an idea!' was his answer to that one.) Was it true that women in India committed suicide on the deaths of their husbands? I could see that all this feigned interest was beginning to please him. He became more and more animated, leaning forward in his chair and cracking the joints of his knobbly fingers as he held forth. Bob yawned and yawned again and gave the puzzle an angry shake, so that the little balls rattled from side to side. Eventually he chucked the puzzle across to an empty chair some way distant from us and picked up a copy of *Tatler*.

He flicked over the pages, then whistled in amazement. 'Look at this! Would you believe it?' He held out the magazine. 'There's Mervyn's mater!' He began to read out the caption in a derisive parody of a county voice. 'The Honourable Mrs Leo Frost, with friend in the Royal Enclosure at Ascot.' The only thing wrong with the county voice was that he pronounced the aspirate of the Honourable, as he always did, in mockery.

[34]

Hands clasped, Mr Williams leaned forward in his chair, revealing those butter-yellow false teeth. 'Is your mother, er, a member of the aristocracy then?' he asked.

'Well, yes – of a sort.'

'Then your father . . .?' He was becoming increasingly excited.

'No. My father's just a plain Mister.'

'His mother's the daughter of a duke,' Bob put in, knowing that this was not true.

'Oh, shut up! Actually, she's the daughter of a peer.' Snob that I then was, I took pleasure in establishing this.

'And what would his title be?'

I told him. 'At least, that's what he was. Grandad's dead now. Ma's – my mother's – cousin is the present Lord. But they don't really get on.'

'He went to prison,' Bob said. 'You must have read about it in the papers. For assaulting a police officer who stopped his car when he was drunk. It wasn't the first time he'd done that. Or been drunk when driving.'

Mrs Williams scowled at her son.

'His mother's grandfather was that General – General Lymot – who gave the order for his troops to fire on that huge crowd in Bhopal,' Bob continued. 'Hundreds and hundreds were killed.'

'I'd no idea you were one of that family,' Mr Williams said. 'Why didn't you tell me all this, Bob?'

Instead of answering, Bob held out the magazine to his father. 'Isn't she a stunner?'

'She's certainly, er, striking,' Mr Williams conceded after a hurried glance.

'But what on earth is she wearing on her head?' Bob now demanded, holding out the photograph to each of us in turn. 'Frost, what on earth is she wearing on her head? It looks like a giant cowpat.'

[35]

'Bob, please!' Angrily, Mr Williams snatched the magazine, snapped it shut and returned it to the pile on the table.

Mrs Williams yawned, placing the back of her hand with its worn wedding-ring and its garnet signet ring up to her pale, narrow lips. 'Deary me! I feel quite sleepy after that excellent lunch. I think that I'll toddle upstairs for a little snooze.'

Bob jumped decisively to his feet. 'I'm afraid we ought to be getting back.'

'Getting back!' Mrs Williams wailed. 'But I thought you could stay out till seven.'

'Oh, no!' Bob lied. 'We have to be back by three thirty.'

'But I thought . . . Are you sure?'

'Absolutely. You see, we have choir practice.' Neither Bob nor I was in the choir.

'You never told us you were in the choir, Bob!' Mrs Williams said.

'Didn't I? Oh, I got in last term. Frost got in as soon as we arrived here – before his voice had broken.'

'Well, that's wonderful news. But it does seem odd to have a choir practice on a Sunday evening when parents are down for the weekend.'

Bob shrugged. 'It's rotten luck.'

'Well, if you have to go, you have to go.' Mrs Williams sighed. Suddenly she looked far frailer and older than before, her shoulders slumped and the corners of her mouth turned down, to emphasise the deep lines on either side of it. 'Then we won't see you before our departure, I suppose?' The next morning they were returning to London. The morning after that they would be off again to India, for another four years of duty.

When the time came for goodbyes, Mrs Williams

[36]

clutched Bob to her, with a gulping moan. 'Oh, Bob, Bob, Bob! These separations! Why, why, why?' Tears began to gush out of her eyes and coursed down her cheeks.

'Well, that's what the Good Lord wants of us,' Mr Williams said, in a tone which suggested that he was not really convinced of this. He put an arm round his wife: 'Now, buck up, Mother.'

Angrily she turned her head round and up and glared at him. There was hatred in that glare. I was amazed and frightened by it.

Out in the yard, where we had left our bicycles, Bob suddenly began to laugh. He laughed on and on, as though in mounting hysteria. Then abruptly he stopped. 'Sorry about that,' he said. 'I just couldn't take any more. There are times when they just don't seem related to me, related to me in any way at all. Do you ever feel that about your mother?'

'No.' There were times when I felt related to her far too closely, bone of her bone, flesh of her flesh.

'There she was blubbing away, and I could feel nothing, nothing whatever. Except an impatience to get away from her. Does that strike you as terribly unnatural?'

It did. But I replied with no more than a shrug. Then asked: 'Are we going back?'

'Of course not, idiot!' He mounted his bicycle and rang the bell once, twice. 'We're going out to Pulverton.'

'To Pulverton!' Why on earth should we be going out to that dank little country town, little more than a long row of thatched cottages surrounded by council estates similar to the ones now surrounding us? 'What are we going to do in Pulverton?'

[37]

'We're going to have tea in the Green Cockatoo. I
you have some money on you, that is. Dad forgot to tip
me and I forgot to remind him.'

'What's the Green Cockatoo?'

'A tea-shop. Where else would we have tea?'

'But why do we have to go there? It's miles and
miles. And it's far too hot for bicycling.'

'Wait and see!'

It was during a Field Day, which had occupied me
along with most of the rest of the boys, that Bob had
first visited the Green Cockatoo. Although he was later
to have a 'good' War as a boffin in the obscure world of
Intelligence, at that time, claiming to be a pacifist, he
had refused to join the OTC. The head monitor, our
housemaster and finally Mr Curry had all tried to
persuade him of the error of his views; but, as so often,
opposition merely made him more obdurate.

'I was cycling past and suddenly, in the doorway
there she was!' At this point, abreast, we were flying
down a hill, in a wind so strong that he had to shout to
be heard.

'Who was?'

'This girl, idiot, this girl! You've never seen anything
like her.'

But when we arrived at the Green Cockatoo, a
thatched cottage in that low jumble of thatched cottages, the 'girl' turned out to be a woman, plump,
placid, with coarse, deeply waved red hair, who must
have been at least thirty. As we placed ourselves at one
table, she was serving another. Bob leaned across our
table to whisper to me: 'That's her. That one' – he made
a gesture with his head – 'not that old hag over there.'
To me both were old hags.

His attempts at flirtation were embarrassingly
clumsy. When the woman asked us: 'Well, what would

[38]

you like?', he leered at her: 'Do you really want to know?' Later, as she set down the tea things, he peered over the V revealed as her cotton dress fell away from her ample breasts, and announced: 'I can see all kinds of wonderful things in the happy valley that I'm sure I ought not to be seeing.'

After more of this, she said in a lazy, good-natured voice: 'Oh, give over, do!' She turned to me: 'Is he always like this?'

I did not know what to answer, having never been with him and a woman who attracted him. I gave an embarrassed laugh.

Suddenly – he had been watching her as she hurried from one table to another – he announced to me in a voice so loud that I feared that everyone must have heard him: 'I've got a cock-stand.'

'Oh, shut up!'

He insisted on our spinning out the tea, now calling for some more cakes and now for some more hot water.

Eventually, the waitress came over with the bill. 'I'll give you this now. I'm about to be off.'

'You're leaving us! How could you be so cruel?'

She gave a resigned sigh. 'Oh, stow it, do!' Then she turned to me. 'Can't you keep him in order?'

Again I gave that embarrassed laugh.

'Where are you going?'

'What business is that of yours, I'd like to know?'

'Don't tell me you're meeting a boyfriend. That would be too cruel.'

She giggled. She was beginning to enjoy the *badinage*. 'That's my secret,' she said.

Once she had vanished, Bob decided that there was no more reason for us to stay there. Disconsolately he got astride his bicycle. 'Oh, fuck! She must have a boyfriend already.'

[39]

'She's not exactly young, is she? She might be married,' I added.

'Oh, fuck, fuck, fuck!'

For a while we bicycled in silence. Then, after we had left the village behind us, he began to curse quietly to himself: 'Oh, fuck! Oh, bugger! Oh, shit, shit, shit!'

'What's the matter?'

'I've got to do something about this cock-stand. She's given me this hellish cock-stand and I can't get rid of it.'

Soon after that, he slowed down, dismounted, and wheeled his bicycle into a copse beside the road. Reluctantly I followed him.

'Look at it! Just look!' He had unbuttoned his fly. Now with a grimace, he held his swollen cock out in his hand for my inspection. I was amazed both by the livid purple colour of its circumcised head and by its size, so incommensurate with his puny stature.

He laughed. 'Don't gape like that! You've seen lots of these before in the showers.' He was right. But since he usually avoided taking the compulsory cold shower every morning, I had never seen his.

'Go on! Give it a tug!' Now he was half leaning against, and half lying on, a grassy bank behind him.

'Certainly not!'

'Then I'll have to do it myself.'

Fascinated, I watched him, while pretending to be totally uninterested. His eyes were screwed up, his mouth parted, with a thread of saliva glistening in the late summer sunlight between the upper teeth and the lower ones. His breath came in gasps from the effort. All at once I felt my own cock harden.

'Oh, oh, oh!' The semen shot out, some landing on my shoe. He began to roar with laughter. 'That was terrific! Te-bloody-rrific!' He rolled the r's of the penultimate syllable in triumph.

[40]

'Look what you've done to my shoe!' I reached for a handful of grass, tore it from its roots and then bent over to wipe away what looked like a gob of phlegm.

Again I heard him roar with laughter. 'There's nothing like a really good wank,' he said. 'But it would have been even better if you'd done it for me.'

Although then almost sixteen years old, I had never masturbated before in my life. But that night, lying in a state of extreme awareness which I found impossible to explain and which kept me awake while all the other boys in the dormitory were sleeping around me, I suddenly found that, unbidden, there came into my mind that image of Bob, half lying on, and half leaning against, the grassy bank behind him, his hand clutching his swollen cock. Perhaps I should try it? Clearly he had derived an intense, if brief, pleasure from the exercise.

Eventually, I got out of bed and, fearful of waking anyone, tiptoed on bare feet down the linoleum-covered passage to the lavatories, three in a row without any doors, at the far end of it. I squatted on the seat, dreading that someone, suddenly afflicted with diarrhoea, might rush down the passage and find me at what I was planning to do. I grasped my cock and began to rub it, at the same time shuffling through one image after another, in search of the right one. I thought of one of the maids, a girl who could not have been more than sixteen or seventeen and who had an excitingly feral odour as she leaned over one to put down or remove a plate; of Jessie Matthews, then not the dolorously overweight woman of later years but a pert gamine, whom I had seen during the previous holidays in *The Midship Maid*; of a photograph in a tattered copy

[41]

of *Men Only*, lent to me by Bob, of a busty, blonde woman in a bathing costume, fondling her toes while seated on a rock. But distressingly my cock refused to stiffen, as it so often stiffened, without my volition, on other occasions. Then, unbidden, an image asserted itself, obliterating all the others. It was of a purple, circumcised cock, grasped in a hand on which the finger-nails were savagely gnawed to the quick; of shut eyes in a screwed-up face which seemed to express agony rather than an extreme of pleasure; of a thread of saliva between upper lip and lower. My cock all at once began to simmer and rise. There was no problem after that.

10

Dr Lazarides, who always looked as though he was in need of a shave and who had thick hair on the backs of his hands and sprouting up around the collar of the tight, white tunic which, summer or winter, he always wore when seeing his patients, looked at me quizzically. By then Noreen had already begun to turn the key in the lock that had for so long kept the Black Box sealed and I had become, as Dr Lazarides would put it, 'surprisingly communicative'. He smiled, revealing his large, white, slightly protuberant teeth. 'More than most people here, you pose a question to which I can really find no answer. I always hope that perhaps one day, you will provide the answer for me.'

'Let me try. What is the question?'

'Well, it's really not so much about what you did as about what you are.' He leaned towards me with a coaxing look on his face. 'What made you what you are? Tell me, tell me.'

'What makes anyone what he or she is?'

Ignoring my riposte, he persisted: 'Did something happen – something seemingly trivial but all-important – during your babyhood or infancy or teens? Or was there some kind of diabolic possession? Or was there a genetic cause?' Head on one side, he stared at me. 'You're such an intelligent man that you've probably put all those questions already to yourself.'

'No, I can't say I have,' I lied.

'I increasingly have the feeling that nature and not nurture is the cause of most of the problems of most of the people here. But in your case can I be sure of that?'

Perhaps he should have been putting his questions to Bob, who in those days would from time to time pay me a visit in my incarceration. After all, it was for his work in the field of genetics that he was eventually to win his Nobel Prize.

About genetics, even as a schoolboy Bob would often hold forth to me. Why, I have often wondered, should that particular subject have so much interested him from so early an age? It was as though he had been predestined to make that, and nothing else, his work of a lifetime, just as it was as though another of my schoolmates, a Jewish boy, had been predestined to make the collection of butterflies his hobby of a lifetime, travelling the world in search of specimens (so I learned recently from a Sunday supplement) into old age.

Now, pondering all this in the darkening shop, I can

[43]

for some reason once again hear Bob asking me: 'Do you know what was the most important discovery in the history of genetic disorders?'

In answer to that question, as to so many of his questions, I shook my head.

'The invention of the bicycle. Once ordinary people could easily travel outside their little villages to marry and fuck and reproduce themselves, there was much less chance of genetic disorders multiplying.'

The curious thing was that, though I had and still have no interest in science, I could listen fascinated as he talked in this way about alleles, mutation pressure, random genetic drift, recessive homozygotes and so forth. He himself, however, became totally bored, yawning, shifting restlessly in his chair, scratching his head or his chin, if I, pursuing my own particular obsession, in turn began to speak about such things as the hollowed knop-ribbed stem of a Verzelini goblet, of a necklace with beads of piqué, or of a baluster-bodied silver vase with hammered finish.

My precocious interest in antiques won me far less credit at Gladbury than his no less precocious interest in genetics. 'I'm afraid that academically he's really rather dim,' my then form-master, Mr Peppard, told Ma with good-humoured bluntness when she asked him how I was doing. Since he was handsome and young, she was in no way displeased. 'Really that doesn't surprise me at all. I was an awful dunce at school. I never managed to pass a single exam – not even my School Cert.'

About Bob, on the other hand, the masters were all grudgingly admiring. They knew already that one day he would be someone of whom Gladbury would be proud.

What none of them even guessed was that one day I

[44]

would be someone of whom Gladbury would be ashamed.

11

I have just sold a four-case lacquer inro which, strangely, I had totally forgotten that I had in my stock and which, even more strangely, I cannot ever remember having bought. An elderly, shabbily dressed man, with a high, stiff collar and a high greyish-green trilby hat, came into the shop and asked in a husky voice: 'Do you mind if I have a dekko?' Time-waster, I thought, wishing that I had the self-confidence to place on my door, like a colleague further down the street, a brusque notice: 'No browsers'. Clearing his throat from time to time, he wandered from stand to stand and show-case to show-case. Then I saw that he was rummaging behind a pile of Staffordshire earthenware dishes, all of them dusty and many of them chipped. He brought out the inro and began to examine it. He looked across at me and smiled. Then he held it out to me as though proffering a gift. 'Pretty,' he said. On one side, in coloured *togidashi*, was a mandarin drake on a river bank, on the other side the mate of the drake swimming in the river. 'Very pretty.' I nodded. Then I took it from him and examined it, as though for the first time. 'It's signed "Kajikawa saku".'

'And who is he when he's at home?'

'Well, the Kajikawa family extends over virtually the whole of the nineteenth century. But I'd place this piece at about 1860. But that's only a hunch,' I added.

[45]

'Pretty. Very pretty,' he repeated. 'It might be just the thing.' He did not specify for what purpose it might be just the thing. 'What, er, price did you have in mind?'

When I told him, he gave a low whistle under his breath. 'Steep, steep,' he muttered. 'But it is pretty, very pretty. I rather think I'd better take it.'

After he had left the shop, raising the high, greenish-grey trilby to me before passing out through the door, I tried to remember the provenance of the inro. Probably, I decided, I had bought it as one of a lot. But it was odd that, when the man had held it out to me, I had seemed to be seeing it for the first time.

Replacing the dislodged Staffordshire plates, I suddenly remembered another inro . . .

'Oh, you're not going to see him again, are you? You saw him last week.'

'Not last week, the week before last. Ten days ago.'

'I don't know why you want to see him.'

'Because he's my father.'

'A fat lot of use he's been to you as a father!'

Ma lay out, in beach pyjamas, on a wicker *chaise-longue* in the garden of the Campden Hill Square house. The window of the drawing-room was open behind her, so that she could hear the Harry Roy orchestra blaring out from the wireless. I wondered how long it would be before either Sir Francis or Lady Bracey looked over the garden wall to complain. Each would usually begin in the same way: 'Oh, Mrs Frost, I don't in the least want to be a nuisance but I wonder if I might ask . . .' On one occasion, truculently drunk, Mother had cut in: 'No, you may not ask! You bloody well may not ask!' Later, remorseful, she had sent me

[46]

round with a note of apology – she had had a migraine at the time, the note explained in her huge, sprawling handwriting; migraines always put her in a filthy mood.

As always, I hated to displease her. Lying out there, with the late afternoon sunlight glinting on the short blonde hair which framed her small, triangular face, she looked like a petulant and unhappy child. I hated to see that Gordon's bottle and the ice bucket on the low table beside her. I hated to see that cigarette between her nicotine-stained fingers or sticking out from a long amber holder. I wished for her sake that she could hear from Tim, much though I detested him.

'Is there anything I can get you before I go?'

'Well, I had hoped that you would play a few games of bezique with me. But never mind, never mind. If you have to see your father, then you have to see him.'

'Don't take it like that. I feel sorry for him.'

'Don't you ever feel sorry for me?'

'Often, often.'

'You don't know what it's like to be given the push. Without a word of explanation. Just like that. Life can be terribly cruel. For me, he was The One and Only. I knew that as soon as I set eyes on him. The One and Only.'

'I know, I know.' I went over to her, I put my hand on her shoulder. 'But he'll come back. You've had other quarrels, you've had worse quarrels and at the end . . .'
I wanted to continue: He has nowhere else to stay. This is too good a berth to give up just like that. How is he going to pay for a room? For food? For the clothes he so much loves?

'That was before this man came on the scene.'

'What man?'

'What man? I don't know his name, I just know he exists. He's an American, and he's staying at the

[47]

Dorchester, and he's just crazy about Tim. A rich old queen! I've spoken to him on the telephone – twice. But he gave no name and Tim refused to tell me.'

'But Tim isn't like – like that, is he?'

'Who knows what Tim is like! He'll do anything for cash.'

In the train out to Walthamstow I kept thinking: She ought to be happy, why isn't she happy? At forty-seven, she was still attractive, she had just been left the house and some money, in fact a lot of money, by Aunt Bertha, she was aristocratic, bright, charming. What had gone wrong? Poor Ma, poor, poor Ma!

'How is your mother?' was Dad's first question.

'Oh, as usual,' I replied. 'Up and down.'

He sighed.

The room, at the top of the tall, narrow house, looked out over a graveyard. On that late summer afternoon, there were a number of garishly dressed women with prams in it, a group of them even squatting on grave-stones while they chatted to each other. From time to time one heard the wailing of a child, eerily attenuated by the distance.

Despite the heat, Dad was in a thick tweed suit, woollen socks, woollen shirt in a Tattersall check, woollen tie. He seemed always to be cold, telling me to shut the window or light the gas-fire even in midsummer; and yet, at the same time, his face always looked flushed and damp and he always smelled of stale sweat.

'You don't happen to have a fag on you?' He held up an empty packet of Woodbines and then screwed it up in a fist. 'Finito!' Since he knew that I was forbidden to smoke both at home and at school, why did he suppose that I might have cigarettes on me? Oh, I should have brought him some, I should have brought him some!

'I can go round to the pub if you like.'

[48]

'Later, later! Sit yourself down.'

There was only one armchair and he was in it, sprawled out, his feet, in their grubby gym shoes, resting on the gas-meter for which he would so often ask me for shillings. There was an upright chair but over it were draped pyjama trousers, a shirt, under-pants. Eventually I sat on the edge of the wide, sagging brass bedstead. We looked at each other.

'Have you been out at all?'

He shifted uneasily and sighed. 'Not for a day or two. The nerves have been playing up again. I went out on Thursday, thought I'd toddle round to the pub, and when I was in the street, suddenly this awful panic overcame me. I really thought I was going to pass out, even kick the bucket. I'm not joking!'

I felt a terrible pity for him. I also felt a terrible rage. Like Ma in the past, I wanted to shout at him: 'Why can't you pull yourself together?', totally failing to realise, as I realise all too well now, that not to be able to pull oneself together can be as incurable a disease as rabies or Aids.

'Perhaps if you came out with me . . .'

'Now?' Even the idea filled him with panic. 'Oh, no, dear boy, no, no! I couldn't face it. Sorry.'

Dad's had been a heroic war. But after the MC and the DSO there had followed the period in 1918 when he had been shut up in a Black Box of his own. Shell-shock, they had called it. Ma had told me how, at his worst, he would tremble as though with ague; wake up screaming; weep inconsolably for, literally, hours on end. 'It was a hideous time. And your arrival on the scene hardly improved things. You were a mistake, of course, darling.'

'So how is your mother?' he asked again. 'Is that nancy boy still hanging round her?'

[49]

'Tim?'

'Is that his name? The chorus-boy.'

'He's not a chorus-boy. He's an actor. An out-of-work actor.'

'What does your mother see in him?'

I shrugged. It was a question which I had often put to myself and been unable to answer.

'I suppose he's good-looking. And young. Your mother has this thing about youth. It's because she's so terrified of growing old. And so terrified of dying.'

'She calls him The One and Only,' I said.

He put his hands over his face. His left leg began to shake up and down with increasing agitation.

Fortunately at that moment there was a knock at the door. Then, without waiting for an answer, good, vague, weary Mrs Pavlovsky put her head around it. 'Sorry to disturb you both,' she said in her thick Russian accent. Her cheek-bones high and her grey eyes slanting, her wide skirt reaching almost to her ankles, and a cloth tied over her head and under her chin, she looked like some babushka from the steppes. 'I was wondering if you'd both like a cup of tea. I've just made some.'

'Well, that's very kind of you, Mrs Pavlovsky,' Dad said. 'Very kind of you indeed.' After she had gone, he turned to me: 'What time is it?'

'Nearly five.'

'Really? As late as that! Oh, then do put on the wireless. It's at the right station. Just flick up the switch.'

'You don't want to listen to anything now. I've come to visit you.'

'Just flick up the switch,' he repeated irritably.

Reluctantly I did as he said; and at once a yapping voice in a foreign language – German, I quickly realised – filled the room.

'Who is it?'

'Who is it? Who is it? Don't you know who that is? That's the man who's going to put paid to civilisation as we know it. That's the man who's going to be the death of us all. That's Mr Hitler, Herr Hitler. You've heard of him, haven't you?' Mouth ajar, he stared at the Pye wireless set, its gleaming wooden front decorated with a sun, its rays spoke-like around it. He might have been staring at Hitler himself.

'Oh, for heaven's sake, Dad! You can't understand a word of that, can you?'

Now his huge, stricken eyes were fixed on me. 'I can understand the hate.'

'You don't have to listen to that gibberish to understand hate.'

'It's all going to happen again. Only this time it's going to be even worse, far worse.'

I jumped up from my chair, strode over to the wireless and doused the yelping. 'Sorry, Dad. Either we have that off or I go. I'm not going to sit here listening to something of which I can't understand a single word.'

Mrs Pavlovsky arrived with two cups of stewed, oversweetened Indian tea on a tin tray. 'Sorry,' she gasped, breathless from the climb up all those stairs. 'Some of its slopped into the saucers.' She set down the cups. 'Were you listening to him again?' she asked Dad in an indignant voice.

'Trying to. But this son of mine wouldn't let me. His Nuremberg speech. Very important.'

'You don't want to waste time on that rubbish. Anyway the newspapers tomorrow will be full of it.'

For a while, facing each other, he in the armchair and I on the hardbacked chair, we were silent, sipping at our cups. Then he said: 'I keep telling her that I like my

[51]

tea weak. But does she take a blind bit of notice? Of course not!' Then he relented: 'Well, I suppose I mustn't complain. After all, I don't pay her to feed me. Or to shop for me. Or to wash and iron my shirts. She's a good old soul. She's had a tough life.'

Again there was a silence.

Then, as he often did, he began to tell me about a dream. The dream was about the trenches and, as confused now in the telling as it must have been in the dreaming, it circled round and round on itself, a deadly snake with its tail in its mouth. '. . . It was Bonzo Grace I was first trying to find, but then I realised that old Bonzo was gone, finished, and so I thought: Then I must find Johnny what's-his-name. Only how was I going to find him with those whizz-bangs coming over and the crump of the shells and so little light . . .?' I wished that he would stop. There was sweat on his forehead, the muscles in his throat were taut.

Eventually, his voice faltered, expired. He had shut his eyes. Then he said, in the voice of a frightened child: 'I don't want to have that dream again, I can tell you.'

But I knew that he would, he would.

Again there was a silence, broken only by one desolate sigh from him, followed by another. His eyes were still closed, as though to shut out something, a ghost from the trenches – or of the trenches – invisible to me. Then he shook himself, sat up.

'I'd almost forgotten! I've got a little present for you. It was your seventeenth last Tuesday, wasn't it?'

'Yes. I wish you'd come to the party.'

'I was planning to come. I honestly was. I got myself all togged out and then, well, you know how it is with me. The thought of that long train journey, miles and

[52]

miles, underground, buried . . . And then all the people . . . And that ghastly nancy boy of hers . . .'

'There weren't all that many people,' I said resentfully. 'And Tim wasn't there.'

'Yes, but I wasn't to know that, was I? And in any case, that train journey . . . Sorry, old boy. It just wasn't on. Though I wanted to be with you and I wanted to have an excuse for seeing your mother.' He staggered to his feet. 'Anyway . . .' He drew a deep sigh. Then he crossed the room and tugged at one of the drawers of the fumed oak tallboy. 'Blast!' The drawer was warped and he had difficulty in jerking it open. He scrabbled in a jumble of underwear and eventually came up with something. 'That's it! It's what they call an inro. You'll know more about the things than I do. Japanese. . . . Well, it was a day when for once, don't ask me why, I was totally free of panic. In fact, I was feeling – as our American cousins would say – like a hundred dollars, even a thousand dollars. The sun was out, the sky was blue, and I thought: Why don't I take myself out for a stroll? Which is what I did.' (Get on with it, get on with it, I was thinking in impatience.) 'Just beyond Cullen's there's this little junk shop. I sometimes drop in, though I don't often buy anything – can't afford to! The woman who owns the place is a lady, you know, oh, yes, very classy. I should guess that things went badly for her and that running a junk shop was the way she decided to keep herself in funds. There are old clothes there – filthy, often stinking – and furniture even more junky than in here . . . And bedclothes . . . Well, while I was poking around, and chatting away to her while I did so – she's quite an amusing old trout – I suddenly saw this inro thing, on a window sill. "Hello, hello!" I said to myself. "I know

[53]

someone who might like that, someone who's just had a birthday." I haggled for a while and eventually I managed to knock down the price by a quid or two. She's tough, but I think she likes me . . . So . . .' He held it out to me. 'What do you think of it?'

My first feeling was one of indignation with the unknown woman who had sold it to him; my second, fury with him for once again being conned. But I hadn't the heart to tell him that the inro now resting in my palm was probably no more than ten years old; that it was not really an inro but a clumsy imitation of one, mass-manufactured for gullible people like himself; that I did not want it, in fact hated it for its crudeness and ugliness and spuriousness. Instead I smiled at him: 'Oh, Dad, how lovely. But you shouldn't have, you shouldn't have!'

'You do like it, don't you?' He looked at me beseechingly, perhaps having guessed what my real feelings might be. 'Don't you?'

'Of course! It's terrific. I've always wanted to have an inro. I bought a netsuke in Portobello Road the other day, with the money that Aunt Hilda gave me for my birthday, but this is the first inro I've ever owned. Thank you. Thank you so much.'

'Now take good care of it. Don't lose it.'

'Of course I'll take good care of it.' I rewrapped it in its tissue paper and put it in the right-hand pocket of my jacket, thinking: But he needs that money. He needs it. Why the hell did he chuck it away? Oh, what a bloody fool!

He was still smiling at me. 'What a lot you know about antiques! I wish I knew a half of what you know. I don't know much about anything,' he added with a rueful laugh. 'The War came too soon for me. And then, after it . . .'

[54]

'Shall I go and get you some fags?' Just as he found it almost impossible to leave this tiny, stuffy room under the eaves, so I now found it almost impossible to stay in it.

'Would you? Would you mind? The only trouble is, I don't seem to have . . .' Clowning it up now, he put on an act of turning out his pockets. 'Pension not due till Monday next.'

'I'll pay. Don't bother.'

I rushed out of the room and raced down the stairs.

I rarely smoked, either illicitly at school, although Bob often did so, or at home when Ma was out. But now, to keep Dad company, I sat down opposite him and lit first his cigarette (he coughed asthmatically as he drew on it) and then one for myself.

'Good, eh?'

I hated Woodbines, with their saccharescent after-taste, even more than I hated other cigarettes. But I nodded. 'Terrific.'

'If it weren't for these' – he held out the cigarette between trembling fingers – 'I sometimes think I'd just pack it in. They reconcile me to the mysterious ways of God.' He laughed; and then the laugh turned into a cough. 'Anyway, they do less harm than the bottle. Somehow the bottle has never had any appeal for me.' He drew pensively on the cigarette; then he asked (I, too, had been thinking of Ma at that moment): 'I hope your mother isn't still, er, overdoing it. Is she?'

I shook my head. 'Not too bad.' But the night before I had had to support her up the stairs to bed, and at breakfast I had seen her, through the glass door to the kitchen – the cook was ill and the maid was away, since it was Sunday – picking up the half-empty gin bottle and gulping from it, while waiting for the toast to be done. I blamed Tim's sudden disappearance.

[55]

Soon after that, I looked at my watch and said that I must go.

'Must you? So soon?'

'I'm afraid so. I said I'd take Ma to the flicks.'

It was a lie. I had merely had enough.

'Next time you come, I'll pay you back for the fags.'

'Don't be silly! You've given me that terrific inro. The fags are a small return.'

Suddenly, he had put his arms round me. He was hugging me to him, his head on my shoulder. Then I felt his body shaking against mine and I knew that he was crying.

'Oh, Dad, please, please!' I felt horribly embarrassed; and the embarrassment made me angry.

'Sorry, old chap.' Like a child, he rubbed his eyes with his screwed-up fists. 'Don't know what came over me. It's being alone like this . . . hopeless . . . helpless . . . missing your mother . . . missing you . . .'

I could stand it no longer. 'Well, goodbye, Dad. I'll try to come next Monday. On Tuesday I go back to school. End of the hols.'

'Goodbye, Mervyn!' He tried to catch hold of my hand; but I ignored that and hurried out on to the landing.

'Goodbye!' I called out. Then I began to race down the stairs.

As I reached the ground floor, the door of Mrs Pavlovsky's sitting-room opened and first her leggy black cat and then she appeared.

'Oh – er – Mr Frost . . . Mervyn . . .' Her cheeks were flushed with embarrassment. 'Might I just have a little word? It's about your papa.'

Oh, lordy, lordy! Was she about to give him notice?

'Yes, Mrs Pavlovsky? I hope nothing is, er, wrong.'

'Well, not really.' She put her head on one side and

[56]

gave me her sweet, silly smile. 'It's just that . . . the rent . . .' Again she put her head on one side, again she gave me that smile, which seemed to be saying: 'Aren't I a fool to bring such a thing up?'

'Hasn't he paid it?'

'Not for three weeks. I need that money. I have all kinds of expenses with this house. I hate to trouble him and I hate to trouble you. But I thought that perhaps you could say something to your mama.'

I began to explain that, in a few days, Dad would be getting his pension. As soon as it arrived, I was sure that he would pay her. That would be his first priority, I said.

'Yes, I'm sure you're right . . . But . . .'

Eventually I drew out the wallet which Ma had given me for my birthday. It still contained some of my birthday money. 'Let me give you something,' I said. I tweaked out a pound note. 'I'm afraid that's really all . . .'

'Oh!' She was reluctant to take it from me. 'I didn't mean that you should . . . That's very good of you, Mervyn. Are you sure you can spare it?'

'Quite sure.'

'Well, in that case . . .' She took the note and tucked it into the pocket of her voluminous skirt. 'I won't say that it's not a relief to have something.'

On the underground train I pulled out the inro, peeled back the tissue paper and examined it again. It was even worse than I had thought. What an idiot he was! Why hadn't he given the money to poor old Mrs Pavlovsky instead of wasting it on something so trashy?

*

[57]

. . . Now I begin to think of my recent purchaser discovering that other inro. Where did it come from? How is it that I have absolutely no recollection of ever having bought it, indeed of ever having seen it before he held it out to me? Could it be that Dad's inro, which I long ago mislaid, God knows how, has undergone a mysterious transformation from an object of no aesthetic or financial value into one of both those things? After all, in the end my relationship with him no less mysteriously transmuted itself into something enduring and precious.

12

After I have skidded my way through the three Sunday papers, I keep returning to the typescript. But Noreen must on no account see it. All the time that she is in the kitchen, busy with the luncheon, I listen for her approach. The desk drawer is out and I have the *Sunday Times* magazine open on my knee. I can quickly push the typescript into the drawer and pretend to be reading the magazine.

Noreen is singing to herself, in that high, clear voice of hers, the voice of a cathedral choir-boy, not of a woman of eighty-three.

'Wo die Rose hier blüht, we Reben um Lorbeer sich schlingen . . .'

It's Wolf, Hugo Wolf, isn't it – 'Anakreons Grab'? I've never really been able to do with Wolf but she loves him. She sounds so happy; and perhaps, since Goethe's poem is about the grave of a happy poet, that is as it should be. But how can I feel happy? It is as though I were sitting with a vial containing some deadly bacillus in my lap, in the knowledge that eventually it will explode from some mysterious pressure mounting within it.

I call out: 'Can't I do something?'

'No, no! Thank you. Everything's under control.'

I know that every movement that she makes in the kitchen – the stooping to open the oven door, the stretching to fetch down the colander – causes her pain. But she wants her independence; and, even more strongly, she does not wish to acknowledge that, at long last, life has got her on the ropes.

Since, after the rain of yesterday and the day before it, it is now sunny and cloudless, we are going to eat in the garden. Once, long before we came to live here, that garden stretched on and on, down to a little stream; but the previous owners, strapped for money, sold all but a little square to neighbours whom, until then, the stream had always kept at a distance from them. The land thus owned by the neighbours, Noreen and I call Naboth's Vineyard. We covet it. We also know, sadly, that we shall never be in a position to buy it back, since we now have so little money and the neighbours have so much.

I hear the heels of Noreen's brogues – except for their smaller size, they are indistinguishable from mine – approaching on the tiles of the kitchen floor, and quickly, in a panic, I thrust the typescript into the drawer, slam the door shut, and then, just as she is entering the room, a tray loaded with crockery and cutlery in her crooked hands, pick up the *Sunday Times* magazine and bend my head to it.

[59]

I look up. 'Oh, I wish you'd left that to me. It's far too much for you.'

She rests the edge of the tray on the desk, with a sigh. The skin under her eyes glistens with sweat, her cheek are flushed. It is too hot a day for cooking. 'What are you reading?'

I glance down, see the photograph. 'Oh, something about that Madonna creature. Not at all interesting.'

She stares at me, with a look of yearning pity. I know that she knows that I am lying. 'Something's on your mind,' she says.

'There's nothing on my mind,' I say tetchily. 'Don't, please, go on about there being something on my mind. Yes, I'm worried about our finances, but when have I not been worried about them? We always pull through. We're not broke, for God's sake.'

She shrugs, raises the tray and hobbles out into the garden. Then I hear her talking to the cat: 'Hello, lovey! Where have you been all morning? I've got some lovely giblets for you. You can have them while we're eating our roast.'

When, eventually, I take the chair opposite to her, she exclaims: 'Oh, what a lovely, lovely day. The forecast got it all wrong. I'm so glad we can eat out. Have you ever seen such roses? It must be because of all that rain.'

She possesses what I have never possessed: a capacity for joy. This joy bubbles up spontaneously, a secret, fresh spring, when one least expects it. She raises her arms, as though to the sun above the trees before her, and smiles, smiles. 'Beautiful, beautiful world!' she exclaims.

Then, miraculously, I too see its beauty, so often hidden from me. The fur of the cat, crouched under a rose bush, is so glossy, and its eyes glitter like mica. I

[60]

can smell the roses frothing above us and, far off, I can hear – is it really possible? – the water of the stream sliding over mossy stones. The bread which she has baked crumbles in my mouth and, soft and cold, I can taste the Normandy butter which I have spread on it. Now I lift my glass. The Bulgarian red was the cheapest in the supermarket; but I savour it on my palate and even relish the sour aftertaste when I have swallowed it.

'I never thought I'd be happy, totally happy, in my eighty-fourth year,' she says. 'Aren't you happy?'

I nod. Yes, like her, I am happy, totally happy.

I have forgotten about that vial of deadly poison secreted in my desk.

13

Bob first met Ma when, at long last, a few months before that seventeenth birthday, she paid a visit to the school. Parents' Days, Speech Day and Sports Day had followed each other and she had never come down for any of them. 'Aren't your parents coming?' my house-master, form-master, Matie (as we called the matron), Bob and the other boys would ask me, their concern toothed with sadism. I would then trot out the excuses which Ma had given me: she had lumbago, she was going to a wedding, she was touring the Greek islands on the yacht of a friend, she must, she just must get to Covent Garden to hear Lotte Lehmann in *Rosenkavalier*.

But what about my father? I would then be asked, to reply, sullenly shifty, that he was also busy. Busy with what, at a weekend? Oh, he often worked at weekends, I would reply. Sometimes the questioner would persist: What exactly was it that my father did? He's in the City, I would say, having heard other boys say the same thing of their fathers.

In fact, Dad was usually alone at the weekends in the huge, cavernous flat in Prince of Wales Drive. (That was before Aunt Bertha had left Mother the house in Campden Hill Square.) By now, his health was better, after he had spent several months at a farm community run by Benedictine monks on the west coast of Scotland. He had gone to bed early and risen early, and had slaved all day at digging, weeding and bedding out, and carrying swill to pigs and hay to cattle. When he had at last returned home, his finger-nails, once so scrupulously kept, were chipped and broken, his lips were chapped, and his face was weather-scarred – 'He looks so vulgarly healthy' was Ma's comment to me. But, although so much better, he would not himself drive the Armstrong Siddeley (crashed twice by Ma) up the spine of England to the school, and he had a terror of travelling in a train, as he had of travelling on the underground.

When Ma did at last come to Gladbury, it was for Founder's Day, and Dad, eventually succumbing to her alternate bullying and wheedling, had agreed to accompany her. Dazed, he stepped out of the car and, jerking in a circle, peered around him. He had himself been a boy at Gladbury, leaving it at the age of seventeen to volunteer for the War. 'Strange, strange,' he muttered.

'What's so strange, darling?' Ma demanded in a steely voice. I knew that she was afraid that he would, as she often put it, 'play up'.

'To be back here. You know . . . so many of the

[62]

people I knew are dead. Gone. Might never have been. Not just boys, beaks also.' He gave a little shiver, then a choking laugh, which was almost a sob: 'A goose must be walking over my grave.'

I was thinking, with surprise: How handsome he looks, how well dressed. His shoes, so often scuffed, had a high polish on them; his suit looked new; and with his shirt, his initials on its pocket, he was wearing a bow-tie. Suddenly I could understand what I had never before understood: how Ma had come to marry him. In contrast, Ma's appearance, in a simple black suit, black court shoes, black pillar-box hat and pearl necklace and ear-rings, was a disappointment to me. Other boys' mothers, in their flowered silks, fur stoles, cart-wheel hats, diamonds, looked so much more striking (a word of approval favoured by Ma herself). It was only later that I learned from the comments of other people that Ma had, in fact, been the most striking woman there. 'That suit must have been Chanel,' my housemaster's wife told me. 'Tremendously chic,' was the comment of another mother, passed on to me by her son.

Still Dad was gazing around him as we walked towards the Chapel. Each year there was a service to commemorate the Founder; after that, there was a luncheon in each house for parents and their offspring. 'Oh, don't be so moony,' Ma hissed at him. Then she linked her arm in mine, making me sway along with her, with Dad behind us.

Mr Curry, dressed in a dark grey pin-stripe suit, all three buttons of which were fastened, a grey-and-white striped shirt with a white stiff collar, and a maroon tie fastened in a tight little knot, approached us at the door to the Chapel. He had never before smiled at me with

[63]

such benevolence. Then, with a similar benevolence, he smiled at Ma. 'You must be Mrs Frost. I've not had the pleasure of meeting you before, have I?'

Dad waited behind us. Mr Curry did not greet him, perhaps did not even notice him there, and Ma made no attempt to draw him in.

'How is my little boy doing?' she asked.

'Not so little! He seems to be shooting up. Oh, sometimes he's a bit dozy, but on the whole we're pleased with him. At least he hasn't got into any scrapes.'

Ma gave her clear, ringing laugh. 'Unlike his mother!'

'I'm sure you've never got into any scrapes, Mrs Frost. I just don't believe it.'

'Oh, yes, I'm afraid I have. Far too many in my day.'

After the heat outside, the Chapel was cool. Dad dropped to his knees and spent a long time praying. After his return from the community, Ma had told me: 'I'm afraid he's got religion in rather a bad way.' She now adjusted her little hat, tweaking at its veil, and then looked around her. 'Who's that boy over there?' she eventually whispered. 'By the pillar.'

'Oh, that's Cowley. The head boy.'

'Very glamorous. He looks at least twenty. Is he a chum of yours?'

'Of course not.' I was overcome with embarrassment. Could anyone have heard her?

Dad, having risen from his knees, coughed and coughed again. I knew that cough so well. Strangely artificial, like the cough of someone who coughs not from compulsion but to attract attention, it always made me uneasy, since it signalled that all was not well with him.

When Cowley began to read the First Lesson, Ma leant towards me to whisper: 'What a wonderful voice!

[64]

So deep . . . I love a deep voice.' She had been fanning herself with the order of service, even though, after the summer heat outside, the Chapel struck me as chilly. Now she ceased to do so. Her lips parted, hands in lap, she leaned forward, listening intently.

Again Dad coughed and coughed again. He put a hand up to his mouth, then raised it to his head and began to stroke his greying hair. He might have been lovingly stroking a cat.

Mr Curry, who had taken Holy Orders, preached the sermon. It was on the theme that the key to the character of the sixteenth-century Founder was that he had been 'every inch a gentleman'. What were the gentlemanly virtues? Mr Curry began to enumerate them.

Suddenly, with what was half a gasp and half a groan, Dad got to his feet and began frantically to push past the other people seated in our pew.

'Excuse me, excuse me,' he kept saying, so loudly that everyone in the Chapel must have heard him. Mr Curry paused, stared down, then resumed. The metal caps on Dad's shoes rang out on the flags like anvil strokes. His noisy progress seemed to go on forever. Ma looked at me, then put a hand over mine. She gave a little smile. 'Don't worry,' she whispered. 'The old claustrophobia – or do I mean agoraphobia? I never know the difference.'

When we emerged from the Chapel, Dad had vanished.

'Oh, this is too bad!' Ma exclaimed. 'I had a feeling that it would be a mistake to let him come with me. He really does have a knack for ruining a day.'

'Perhaps he's by the car.'

'Oh, I doubt it.'

'Well, let's go and see.'

I had been right. There he was, squatting on the running-board, his knees all but touching his chin and his head in his hands.

'You'll get that suit filthy,' Ma said, as we approached him.

He looked up. His eyes were bleak with despair. 'Sorry. Just couldn't take it.'

'Well, never mind! But we'd better get over to this luncheon party. If I know anything about boys, there'll be no food left unless we hurry.'

'I'll wait here.'

'Nonsense! You'll come along with us.'

'No, I can't, I can't. The thought of all those people . . . I'll just pass out. That's all.'

'Oh, don't be so childish! . . . Oh very well! Do what you like! But what are you going to do with yourself?'

'I'll sit in the car.'

'But you'll come with us to the concert this afternoon, now won't you?'

He groaned. 'No, no!'

Mother looked at me, shrugged her shoulders and once again adjusted the veil of the little hat. 'Then where shall we meet you?'

'Here. I'll be sitting in the car.'

'But this is ridiculous! You can't sit for the best part of the day in the car. You'll be boiled alive in this heat.'

'I'll be sitting in the car,' he repeated.

'As you wish, as you wish.' Ma opened her crocodile leather bag and took out the car keys. 'Here are the keys. Now don't lose them. Don't lose them!' She might have been talking to me when I was still a child.

'I won't lose them.'

'Promise?'

'Promise.'

The luncheon was out in the garden of the house. It

was only on such occasions that the boys ever entered, since at other times it was reserved exclusively for the use of the housemaster, Mr Philby, his plump, placid wife and their boisterous twin girls. Often, bored with my prep, I would get up from my study desk and go to the window. Sometimes, Mrs Philby, a keen gardener, would be weeding there. More often, the seven-year-old twins would be playing some rowdy game, which involved a lot of chasing and wrestling and usually ended in tears for one or other or both of them.

May as always, became the centre of attention. She was so carefree, so self-possessed, so entertaining that no one present could have guessed at those squally moods when she would scream abuse at Dad, the daily or me, would retire to bed with a glass and a bottle of gin, or would hiss angrily down the telephone to some boyfriend who had neglected her or some woman friend who had disagreed with her. Many women were standing for a lack of anywhere to sit. But it was for Ma, so much younger-looking, that an elderly man, admiral grandfather of a classmate, at once tottered up to offer his chair.

'That's terribly kind of you,' Ma said, 'but I wouldn't dream . . .'

'No, no, dear lady!' he cut in. 'I wouldn't dream of your standing for a moment longer.'

With a dazzling smile, Ma lowered herself into the vacated chair. She turned to me. 'That's gallantry for you!'

'Let me get you something to eat and drink,' the admiral volunteered.

'Oh, my son will do that. Mervyn, be an angel . . . I saw some cold salmon and salad . . . And a glass of white wine.'

[67]

When I returned, riskily balancing a glass of white wine for her on one plate of salmon and a glass of lemonade for myself on another, she was talking now merely to the admiral but to three other men as well. Ho, ho, ho, the admiral was laughing, his previously red face now purple; and the others then all joined in in more restrained fashion. 'Of course you know what Thelma Furness once said about the Prince . . .' I myself knew, having already been told by Ma: Thelma Furness had told Ma that, in bed with the Prince of Wales, it was a case of an awfully little having to go an awfully long way. It amazed me that she should venture on something so *risqué* with a group of men totally unknown to her. But at the conclusion there was even more laughter.

Mother took the plate and glass from me, without a word of thanks. Then she peered up at me. 'Oh, dear I've shocked my little boy. Look how pink he's gone!'

I went even pinker, as the others all guffawed.

It was then that Bob appeared. Since his parents were now back in India and since he had (as far as I could judge) no relatives remotely interested in him, he was one of the few boys to be all on their own on that day. As the adults all guffawed, so did he, thus making me notice him for the first time.

I scowled at him, and he then smiled back. 'Introduce me.'

I continued to scowl.

'I think your friend wants to meet me,' Ma said.

Reluctantly I said: 'This is Williams, Ma.'

Bob stepped boldly forward and extended a hand. As always, his trousers were at least an inch too short, so that between them and his scuffed shoes his woollen socks were visible. There was an ink smear on the side of his chin and a bristle of blond hair along his upper

p. 'Pleased to meet you, Mrs Frost,' he said in a loud, old voice. It was something that Ma had taught me never to say.

Ma took his hand. 'Pleased to meet you too,' she said, all too obviously mocking him with the repetition. Then she turned to me: 'Have you told me about him?'

'Yes.'

'Is he the one whose parents are missionaries?'

'That's right.' I was feeling more and more uncomfortable. I knew that she was capable of hurting Bob and I did not want him to be hurt.

'I don't think I've ever met a missionary outside the pages of Somerset Maugham. And he makes them sound so dreadful.'

Bob began to laugh. So far from being hurt, he was clearly delighted. 'When my parents next come home, you must meet them,' he said.

'Are they going to come home soon?'

'Not for at least three years.'

'Oh, that's a relief! I was afraid you were going to say that they were coming home next week.'

Again, instead of being annoyed or hurt as I had expected, Bob laughed in delight.

'Aren't you eating?' Ma asked.

'Later.'

'I don't imagine there'll be any food left later.' She picked a tomato-half out of her salad and held it out between thumb and forefinger. 'Eat this, at any rate, to stave off the pangs.'

Bob lowered his large, round head and took the piece of tomato between his teeth.

Now, clearly irritated by Bob's interruption, the admiral said: 'Where on earth did you get your hair cut like that?'

'Do you like it? I cut it myself.'

[69]

'No, I do not like it! I must say most of the boys her look far scruffier than in my day. We'd be beaten if w didn't clean our shoes,' he added, staring down a Bob's scuffed ones.

Again Bob laughed.

Ma now lost interest in him. She did not speak t him, she did not glance at him, as she resumed he conversation with the men gathered around her.

'You'd better get yourself something to eat,' I tol him. 'I could do with more of this salmon myself.'

Bob seemed not to hear me, as he listened attentivel to Ma's *badinage*.

'Bob!'

'Oh, okay. But I don't feel all that hungry.'

As we wove our way through the crowds to the lon tables on which the food and drink were set out, h said: 'She's even better than her photograph. Super! can't imagine how she ever produced a twerp like you In any case, she doesn't look old enough.'

'She's over forty,' I said. His enthusiasm had mad me feel jealous.

'I don't believe it!'

'Years over forty.' Only later did I realise, with pang of guilt, that I had been terribly disloyal to Ma She was often telling me: 'Now remember, darling, m age is an absolute secret between us!'

Bob was only half-way through his plate of food when Mr Philby interrupted. 'Oh, Williams, you're o your own, aren't you? I mean, you haven't got anyon down, have you? I wonder if you can nip over to th assembly hall to help out with the chairs. They seem t be short-handed.'

Bob put down his plate with a grimace of annoyance 'Oh, fuck!' he exclaimed, while Mr Philby was still i earshot. Startled, Mr Philby looked over his shoulder, almost returned to us, and then decided to move on.

When people began to trickle out of the garden, on their way to the concert, Ma said to me: 'You won't mind, will you darling, if I give this concert a miss? The admiral wants me to see the yacht he's just bought. It's anchored in the estuary.'

If he invited her to see the yacht, why did he not invite me to see it too? I felt chagrined.

'Oh, all right,' I muttered, trying to be offhand.

What time would they be back? she then asked the admiral, who answered: 'Oh, not too late, not too late. Our crowd has to get back to London tonight.'

'Well, so have I,' Ma said. I noticed that it was 'I' not 'we', although Dad would be travelling back to London with her.

Eventually alone, I looked around for Bob, but I could nowhere see him. He must still be at work with the chairs. Disconsolate, I wandered out and began to trudge in the direction of the assembly hall, where the concert was to take place. Then, all at once, I thought of Dad, brooding alone in the car, with nothing to eat. I retraced my steps back into the garden, now deserted except for three waitresses and a single group of adults – a man in a hammock, two women, flushed with heat, on a bench – and a small boy, a newcomer that term to the school, lying out on the grass beside them.

I picked up one of the paper plates and surveyed what was left of the food. Poor Father! He was not going to have much of a meal. There was a scrawny chicken leg, some limp lettuce leaves at the bottom of a bowl, some potato salad, a crust of French bread.

'Haven't you had something to eat already?' The voice was accusatory. I looked round. It was Mrs

[71]

Philby, her face flushed and beads of sweat glistening along her upper lip, no doubt as much from the social strain of the occasion as from exertion and heat.

'This is not for me, Mrs Philby. It's for my father.'

She looked around the garden. 'And which is your father?'

'He's not here. He's sitting in the car. He has a migraine.' I had remembered how often Ma used the excuse of a migraine for not doing what she did not want to do.

'Oh. Oh, I'm sorry.' She was sympathetic. 'I'm a terrible sufferer from migraine myself. Would he like two of the pills I take, do you think? Ergotamine. I find them marvellous.'

'Oh, no, thank you. I think he has some pills of his own.'

Dad lay along the back seat of the car, his knees drawn up and his eyes shut. He looked completely relaxed and at peace after all his earlier turmoil. I opened the door. It seemed a shame to wake him. Then I said: 'Dad,' and repeated it more loudly, 'Dad.'

With a cry of terror his legs shot down to the floor and his torso shot up. 'What . . . what the hell . . .?' He squinted up at me, as though I were a thief. Then he gasped: 'Oh, you!'

'I've brought you some grub. It's the best I could do. What was left.'

'Well, that was very thoughtful of you, old chap. Very thoughtful.'

I handed him the paper plate. 'There were strawberries and cream. But I couldn't carry them as well. I could go back later for them,' I added, not in the least wishing or intending to do so.

'No, no. This is ample.'

To my surprise he began to eat with gusto.

Then he looked up: 'What's happened to your mother?'

At all costs, I must shield both her and, more important, him. 'Oh, I think she met some people she knows. They wanted her to see their yacht.'

'Why didn't they want you to see it?' Had he guessed that I was lying?

'I don't know.'

His meal over, I asked him: 'What would you like to do now? You don't want to sit here all afternoon, do you?'

To my amazement he said: 'Why don't we toddle along to this concert? It's Keith Faulkner, isn't it? I've always liked his voice.'

I looked at my watch. 'It'll already have started.'

'Oh, that doesn't matter, does it? We can creep in.'

Remembering the noise which he had made when quitting the Chapel, I was dubious. But I merely said: 'Oh, all right.'

Surprisingly, he took a seat at the back of the hall with no noise at all. I sat down beside him.

Keith Faulkner was singing; and what he was singing was Wolf's 'Anakreons Grab', then heard by me for the first time. My life, like a cavernous room, has been full of such echoes, ricocheting back and forth, back and forth. I often wonder if in other people's lives the same thing happens.

After the concert, we returned to the car to wait for Ma's return. For a while Dad was silent, his hands resting on the steering wheel and his gaze unfocused as he stared out ahead of him. Beside him, I was

[73]

bored. I wished that he would say something. I wished that I had the energy and interest to say something myself.

Then he said: 'I can never really do with Wolf. The one for me is Schumann, Robert Schumann. Always has been. You know, in the trenches we had this chap, Freddy Noakes, and he'd been training in Germany to become a Lieder singer. He would sing for us. I think he might eventually have become famous but . . . Well, he was one of the first to go. One of the things he sang was "*Dichterliebe*". Marvellous.' For a moment he was silent; then he put his head on one side and softly began to sing:

'Im wunderschönen Monat Mai . . .'

He completed the first two stanzas, the pitch impeccable. I had never before heard him sing. I had never known him to show any interest in music, as Ma did with her frequent visits to Bayreuth, Glyndebourne and Covent Garden. There was a beauty in the soft-grained tenor voice; and all at once he himself looked beautiful, his face serene, even happy, instead of tense with anxiety or haggard with despair.

When he had finished, I cried out: 'Oh, do sing something else, Dad! Please!'

He shook his head.

'Please!'

'How about this then?' He began not so much to sing as to croon '*Schöne Fremde*':

'Es rauschen die Wipfel und schauern . . .'

When he had finished, he said: 'I love those last two lines. Did you understand them?'

[74]

I laughed. 'No, Dad. I don't know any German. You know that.'

'Well, how can I translate them for you? The title is, yes, "A Beautiful Foreign Land", and in those last two lines Eichendorff looks forward to some great happiness – "the distance speaks with ecstasy of some great happiness to come." Yes, that's more or less it.' He turned to me. 'But what is that great happiness to come? Does he mean love? Does he? Freddy Noakes thought he did. But I think that he really means death. Death is the great happiness to come. Death is the beautiful foreign land.'

I heard voices approaching, and then there was a tap on the window beside me. It was Ma tapping with her long, painted nails. Behind her were the admiral and two other, younger men. 'Sorry to be so late, darlings,' she trilled. 'But the estuary turned out to be much farther than we'd imagined.'

Dad clambered out of the driver's seat to make way for her.

After they had gone, I walked round the cricket field, alone. I could still hear Dad singing '*Schöne Fremde*' in that beautiful light tenor of his. I had felt very close to him, I still felt very close to him. It was the first time that I realised that I loved him more than I loved Ma.

In the dormitory, Bob sat on my bed. Since he often could not be bothered to wash, his feet were grubby and smelly, and there was still that ink-stain on his chin. He swung the feet back and forth, grinning with happiness.

'She's terrific. Super. I wish I had a mother like that.

[75]

Why does mine have to be so old? Ancient. And she wears such ghastly clothes. And she never has anything interesting or amusing to say.'

As he went on, I felt increasingly shocked. I had never before heard anyone talk about his mother in that way – as though she were no closer to him than Mrs Philby or Matie or one of the maids.

'You are lucky! You really are! And the sad thing is that you just don't realise your luck.'

14

I was eight.

Dad was, as so often, absent from the flat in Prince of Wales Drive, taking a water cure in Italy. Ma was paying for it – perhaps, I now realise, not so much because she had hopes of a cure for him but because she wanted him far away.

'What's the matter with Dad?' I asked her in the taxi, after we had seen him off at Victoria Station.

She pondered, no doubt trying to decide what it was best to tell a child of my age. 'Well, he had a dreadful time in the War,' she said. 'A lot of his pals were killed and he was almost killed a number of times. They call it neurasthenia. That's what they call it. Neurasthenia.'

'Neurasthenia.' I repeated the strange word with difficulty. I had never heard it before. It is not a word one hears often now.

Soon after that, while Dad was still away, Ma told me that she had to go into a nursing home for 'a little op'. It was left to Aunt Bertha, then still alive, to take charge of me for four days, in the house, overcrowded with vast pieces of Victorian furniture and no less vast portraits of her dead husband's ancestors, in Campden Hill Square. Having never had any of her own, she had no idea how to deal with children. In consequence, I spent most of the time either in the kitchen, with the staff, or in the sombre library, its curtains always closed for fear that the sun would bleach the books, leafing through bound copies of the *Studio*. Could it have been then that I first became interested in antiques?

'What exactly is the matter with Ma?' I asked Aunt Bertha, as I previously had asked Ma about Dad, during my first luncheon at the long, narrow mahogany table, each of us seated at either end, as Aunt Bertha and Uncle Jack used once to be seated.

Aunt Bertha pursed her lips and, raising the jewelled, heart-shaped watch pinned to her blouse, examined it, her chin drawn in. Then, after another pursing of the lips followed by a sigh, she eventually said: 'Oh, it's one of those women's things. Don't worry about it. Nothing of importance.'

Years later I decided that, under the pretence of a D & C, Ma had probably gone into the nursing home for an abortion.

It was during this operation that she met a young Irish doctor always known to me merely as Fergus. With reddish hair, cropped close and sticking up around his wide, freckled face, muscular shoulders and thighs (he was a strenuous but not particularly skilled Rugby football player) and hands which seemed over-large even for someone of his height, he could not have been described as handsome. Having only just qualified, he was at least ten years younger than Ma.

Ma described him to me as 'a rough diamond' after

the three of us had been on an excursion to Hampton Court. He had sat for much of the boat trip with his arm around her, both of them paying me so little attention that by the time we arrived I was sulky and close to tears. But then, all at once, he became interested in me. We must try the maze, he said; and leaving Ma at the entrance – 'No,' she said irritably, 'I've no interest at all in going round it, I'll just sit here and wait for you' – he grabbed my hand and pulled me in. We then jogged, rather than walked, up and down the narrow paths in so short a time that he must, I realise now, have been there before and solved the mystery of the layout. Later, he showed me the real-tennis court and the vine. When we had luncheon in the hotel, he insisted that I should follow a vast Pêche Melba with an even vaster Poire Hélène, thus ensuring that I felt sick for most of the rest of the day.

How could Ma have fallen in love with someone so plain, so inelegant, so penurious, and (as she herself described him, using a word nowadays taboo) common, mystifies me. But perhaps what attracted her was precisely these things. All her previous lovers had had no such disadvantages.

During this 'friendship' (to me she always referred to her lovers as friends) with Fergus, Ma also continued to see Noel Bartholomew, who was a junior minister, who was married, and who had extensive estates on the Borders. At that time I always thought of him, with his grey, carefully groomed hair and grey moustache, his aquiline nose covered with a frayed network of red and purple veins, and his wheezing laugh, as old; but I realise now that he could not have been much more than fifty, since he survived, eventually a peer, into the era of Macmillan. In those days a minister had to be even more discreet than today; but Ma and Uncle Noel

[78]

(as she insisted that I call him) were assisted in their liaison by the fact that his wife, having absolutely no taste for metropolitan life, spent almost all her time in the country with her horses and her 'Staffies' (as Uncle Noel called them).

Ma was soon faced with a quandary. Uncle Noel was to leave for New York on the *Queen Mary*, to take part in an economic conference. Since his wife had no intention of accompanying him, he had put it to Ma that she should come instead. I presume that he was willing to pay all her expenses; but, even if he had not been, she could, at that period, have afforded herself to pay for them. Unfortunately, at the same time, Fergus was planning to take some leave, and had suggested to Ma that they should go together to Spain.

'Oh, dear, I just don't know what to do,' she complained to me more than once, until I said: 'Why don't you do neither? Then just the two of us could go away for a holiday.' Her response was a sharp: 'Oh, don't be such a nitwit!'

Coming to say goodnight to me before going to the theatre with Uncle Noel, she yet again reverted to the subject. 'He'll want to know what I've decided. And I've still decided nothing. It would be lovely to see New York again and I've always wanted to travel on the *Queen Mary*. And I might get to meet the President – Uncle Noel is related in some distant way to him. On the other hand, Fergus would be more fun. Don't you think he'd be more fun?'

'Yes, I think you should go with Fergus, Ma.' I much preferred the younger man to the older.

She hugged me to her with extraordinary enthusiasm. 'Oh, darling, I think you're right, I think you're absolutely right. I should always ask you for your advice, when I'm torn between two boyfriends.'

[79]

'If you do go with Fergus, what . . . what will become of me?'

Clearly she had never given this problem a moment's thought. 'Well, I suppose you could come with us. Though I'm afraid it might all be terribly boring for you. Or you could go to stay with Aunt Bertha. Since Uncle Fred died, she's been terribly lonely, in that big house with only the servants to keep her company.'

'Oh, Ma, do let me come with you! Do! Please! Please!' Suddenly I was frantic.

'Well, I must think about it. And discuss it with Fergus. Whether he would want you along, I just don't know.'

Night after night in Barcelona, Ma and Fergus would go out and leave me alone in the Ritz Hotel bedroom. (Ma, I realise now, must have been paying for everything, or almost everything.) Sometimes a jolly, large-bosomed maid, with a rudimentary knowledge of English, would whisk in on her round of duties and chat to me. On one occasion she brought me a toy: a hen, carved out of wood, which went through the motions of pecking for invisible grain, bobbing up and down, if I tugged on a string. On another occasion, she and I guzzled a huge bar of Toblerone chocolate given to me by Fergus.

I always used to wake when, through the locked communicating door between my bedroom and theirs, I heard Ma and Fergus return, with a lot of chatter and laughter. Once or twice I called out for Ma. But either she did not hear me or she decided to ignore me. Once, after that, when I had continued to stay awake, I heard gaspings and moans. What were they doing? I was simultaneously bewildered, frightened and excited by these sounds. I somehow knew that I must never ask either of them, or anyone else, about them.

On the day before our return, I awoke at dawn with an overwhelming feeling of desolation and dread. I have no idea what caused it. I had been perfectly happy when I had gone to bed the previous night. I clambered out of bed and went over to the window. The street lamps were still alight, even though there were smears of orange and red across the bottom of the sky. The square was empty but for a single man with a cumbersome suitcase, trudging diagonally across it. A truck rattled past on the road below. That feeling of desolation and dread intensified. It became an unendurable pain.

I crossed to the communicating door and knocked, first softly, then, gathering courage, as loudly as I could. There was no response. I tried the handle but, as usual, the door was locked. I sat on the edge of my bed, chin in hands, and wondered what to do. I had no notion of the time but I knew that it would be ages before Ma or Fergus stirred. Then I reached a decision. I jumped up from the bed and hurried out into the corridor. I knocked on the door of their room. Again there was no answer. But when I pushed down the handle, to my amazement I was able to enter. The previous night they must have forgotten to turn the key.

I saw what I thought at first was only one person under the bedclothes. Then I realised that it was the two of them, sleeping, limbs inextricably entangled, their bodies glued together. I ventured nearer and nearer.

'Ma! . . . *Ma!*'

Suddenly she started up, a hand to her forehead. The sheet fell away and I saw her naked shoulder and the naked curve of her breast. I let out a wail and threw myself on her, sobbing: 'Oh, Ma, Ma, Ma!'

'What on earth is the matter? What are you doing here at this hour?'

I wanted her to hug me but, so far from doing so, she was trying to push me off her.

'I was frightened. I was frightened, Ma. I awoke feeling . . .'

'What *is* all this nonsense? What were you frightened about?'

Now Fergus awoke. He, too, sat up. His chest, with the red pelt on it, was bare. 'What on earth's going on?'

'This wretched brat barged in a moment ago. He says he's frightened.'

Unlike Ma, Fergus was always kind to me. He put an arm round me. Then he asked me, gently, not in Ma's furious voice, what had frightened me. I replied that I did not know.

'Do you want to get into bed with us?'

'Oh, Fergus, please!' Ma protested. 'He's got to go back to his room.'

'No, let me stay, let me stay!'

Fergus laughed. 'Let him stay.' He lifted the bed-clothes. 'Hop in!'

I snuggled up between them, feeling the warmth of their bare bodies on either side of me. Soon both were once more asleep. But I lay there, eyes open.

I was full of happiness, of a kind that I had never known before.

15

I had recently celebrated that seventeenth birthday. Bob had celebrated his three months before.

'Haven't you got any relatives at all?'

Bob shook his head. 'My father's father is potty. He's in a bin for old people somewhere in Yorkshire. Well, not exactly a bin, a home, run by some churchy organisation or other. The other grandparents all died years ago. That's one of the disadvantages – one of the many disadvantages – of having ancient parents. My mother had a brother but he went off to Australia ages before I was born and nobody seems to know what happened to him.'

I felt sorry for Bob. Although we were the same age, I also now felt protective of him. This was strange, since it was usually he, so much more dominant, who was protective of me.

For the Christmas holidays, he had been at a 'holiday home' in Bexhill, run by a retired Indian Army major and his wife. 'I learned from them,' Bob said, 'that to be kind and to be generous are not the same thing.' They were, he went on to explain, extremely kind people; but they were also extremely stingy ones. There was seldom enough to eat for the eleven boys and girls in their care; and such was the inadequacy of the heating of the rambling house during an exceptionally harsh winter that Bob returned to Gladbury with chilblains so severe that they were constantly bleeding. 'They should have made you wear mittens,' Matie said, providing him with a pair. It is now years since I saw chilblains on anyone; but in those days, when only the rich had central heating, they were all too common.

Bob began to tell me of one of the girls at the home. Although only eleven, she was 'terribly sexy – with breasts, real breasts.' She was 'ready for anything'; he and she used to hide in a garden shed and 'play' with each other. Prudishly, I wanted to hear no more. 'Oh, shut up! Shut up! It's disgusting. You'll get yourself into awful trouble if you go on like that.'

The next holidays, the Easter ones, Bob's parents arranged for him to spend with one of the masters, Mr Graham, his pregnant wife and five children on a farm in Staffordshire. When I told Ma about Mr Graham's many children – having seen him once at a Parents' Day, she had said to me that he was 'really rather handsome in a Heathcliffe sort of way' (I then had no idea who Heathcliffe was) – she remarked that 'someone should tell him about birth control.' I passed this on to Bob, who replied: 'No good. He's a Roman Catholic.'

The farm, which was owned by one of Mrs Graham's cousins, was swept by icy winds, and so isolated that for Bob to go into Stoke-on-Trent involved a long ride by bus. The Grahams, thoroughly uxorious, tended to neglect even their own children, who ranged in age from two to eight. In Bob and his doings they had absolutely no interest at all. 'The only time they ever paid any attention to me was when they wanted me to take charge of one of their kids.' He stared out of the study window, his face dark with anger. Then he sighed: 'I was glad to get back to this place, I can tell you! And I never expected to say that.'

It was then that the idea came to me. 'I must ask Ma if you can spend the next holidays with us.'

[84]

'Are you daft?'

'Not at all. Why not? She's been talking of renting a house on Lake Como. It would be super! She usually has a boyfriend with her and I spend most of my time on my own. If you were there . . .'

Bob still looked dubious. Perhaps he did not really believe me. 'To be with your mother for the whole holidays . . . And with you,' he added as an after-thought. All at once his face blazed with pleasure. 'Oh, that really would be terrific!'

16

Ivor Wilkinson, who lives in the large, square red-brick house, built by himself, at the top of the street, tele-phoned this morning. It was typical that he would not tell Noreen what he wanted, but should ask for me, even though I was then in the bathroom. Although he would indignantly deny it, his is a world in which men are the chiefs and women are the coolies.

'Oh, Maurice . . . Is this an inconvenient moment? I always forget that most people don't get up as early as we do.' He wanted, he said, to discuss 'something rather delicate with you – with Noreen and you,' he hastily corrected himself.

'What's it all about?'

'Well, shall we postpone my telling you until our meeting?'

Eventually, we agreed that he and his wife, Claudine, should come round for a drink after dinner.

Both of them are pillars of our church, Ivor as a

churchwarden and Claudine as an arranger of everything from flowers for the altar to an expedition for the
old people to see Danny La Rue in pantomime in
Brighton. Recently, they exerted themselves to raise
money for a Croatian village, with an outcome which
caused indignation to them and amusement to us and
our friends.

Three or four years ago, they were motoring up from
Athens through what was then Yugoslavia when, in a
remote mountain village, their car broke down. Since
there were no spare parts and no professional
mechanic, they were stuck there; and since there was
no hotel or even inn, they had to rely on a village family
to put them up. They returned home full of praise for
the kindness lavished on them. 'They boiled innumerable pots of water so that I could have a bath,' Claudine
said of their hosts, and Ivor then described how, for
want of a suitable electric plug anywhere else, he had
been allowed to shave in the police station.

Subsequently, they were horrified to read in the
Telegraph that this same village had been virtually
destroyed by Serbian guerillas. At once they set about
raising money. Inevitably, since they are extremely
energetic and extremely strong-willed, they soon
enlisted the help not merely of Noreen and me but of
everyone who attends our church and many people
who don't. There was a bring-and-buy sale, a number
of raffles, a concert. Eventually, they had raised a sum
of over two thousand pounds.

The money having been despatched, they were eager
to see how it had been spent. Everyone warned them
of the danger but, undaunted, they set off. Having
eventually arrived in the ravaged village, they were
enthusiastically greeted by all its notables. Everyone
was grateful to them, they would always be remem-

[86]

bered as benefactors, they were constantly told. To what purpose, they at length asked, had the money been put? (Their assumption had always been that it would have been used to rebuild houses, to repair the extensively damaged church, or to evacuate children to a place of greater safety.) The head man of the village beamed. He would show them, he said.

They were taken out on to the steps of the wooden village hall. Then a vehicle slowly passed before them. It was a magnificent horse-drawn hearse, its mahogany and brasswork gleaming. That was what their efforts had bought for the little village, they were told. Now everyone, however poor, could have a slap-up funeral.

When they returned home, Ivor and Claudine were full of indignation – 'Can you imagine the waste, the stupidity?' one or other of them kept protesting. But Noreen told them, bluntly, not to be so silly – 'If you give people money, then you must allow them to spend it as they want.' They were not convinced.

Now we are both wondering if their visit has anything to do with this (for them) fiasco.

'What would you like to drink?' I have again forgotten that both of them not merely do not drink but disapprove of others doing so. Quickly I add: 'There's coffee or tea if you like. Or would you rather have some juice?'

'Juice will be fine,' Ivor says.

'Anything not to give you any trouble,' Claudine adds. Like many people who constantly give one trouble, she often says that.

When we have our glasses of apple juice, Ivor says: 'Well, I think I'd better get to the point.' Then he turns to Claudine: 'Unless you'd like to tell them.'

'No, you go ahead, dear.'

Ivor, who is the boss of our local building firm, is said to have started life as an ordinary labourer. Before she married him, Claudine worked for many years in the local hairdresser's. They are, as Noreen often reminds me, good people; but like many good people, they can be extremely tiresome.

Ivor begins to explain: 'It's really about the vicar. One doesn't wish to pay attention to scandal – does one? – but at the same time, if the church is going to suffer . . .'

'Are you talking about Mrs Wandley?' Noreen interrupts, with her usual bluntness.

'Well, er, yes. I'm sure you know what people are saying.'

'I don't believe a word of it. James is just being kind to her, that's all. He's sorry for her.' Only last year Eric Wandley died of cancer, leaving his wife with three teenage children and virtually no money.

'I only hope you're right.' Claudine sips demurely from her glass. 'But he does seem to spend an awful lot of time over at Wren Cottage.'

I put in: 'Iris Wandley is emphatically not the sort of woman with whom a man has an affair.' Both of them look at me. I know that, for some unfathomable reason, I have shocked them. I want to go on: She's dowdy, she's middle-aged, she has legs like tree trunks, and her nose is always red. But somehow I think that it would be better not to do so.

Ivor shifts uneasily in his chair and gives a small, lady-like cough. He is a big man; but his tweed suit, in a boldly patterned check, light blue on grey, and his brogue shoes both seem too large for him. 'You're a man of the world, Maurice,' he says. 'We're all old enough to know the score in such matters. You must admit it's odd that Jack should visit her every day and

[88]

that he should often visit her for an hour or even more than an hour at a time.'

'How do you know all this?' Noreen demands.

'Well, Mrs Shipman . . .' Mrs Shipman cleans for Ivor and Claudine. 'She lives next door to Mrs Wandley. She can't help seeing what goes on.'

'Just a lot of idle chatter,' Noreen says briskly.

'Well, one would certainly like to think that,' Claudine says. 'I just hope that you're right. As a matter of fact, Mrs Shipman isn't one for idle chatter,' she continues. 'Quite the reverse.'

'Anyway, there's nothing we can do about it,' I say.

Ivor leans forward, his chair creaking under his weight. 'That's the point. That's why I – we – wanted a word.'

'What do you mean?'

'Jack respects you,' he says. 'And likes you. As you know, he and I had that little argy-bargy and things have never really been quite the same between us since.' The 'little argy-bargy' took place when the vicar, desperate to raise money for repairs to the roof of the church, announced that he was proposing to sell a seventeenth-century Dutch silver communion plate by Sigismund Zachammer, the bequest of a recently dead parishioner, and asked me whether I would handle the sale. Ivor, who had known the parishioner in question, had successfully opposed the plan. 'If you were to have a friendly word . . .'

I shake my head vigorously. 'Out of the question.'

'I don't mean that you should accuse him . . . You're a tactful man, Maurice. You could say that you've heard this gossip which you know is only gossip . . . But that you're worried about Mrs Wandley's reputation and his reputation . . .'

'And worried for the church,' Claudine puts in.

'He'll take the hint,' Ivor says. 'From you he'll take it. As I say, he respects you.'

'As we all do,' Claudine says. 'Even if there's nothing in it, he'll be rather more careful about how often he makes his visits and for how long.'

'Sorry. It's not on. If you really think that something should be said to him, then you must say it, Ivor. Or you, Claudine.'

Used to getting their own way in the village, they are both clearly miffed.

'Sometimes I just don't understand you,' Ivor says.

'You're the one to do it,' Claudine persists.

When at last, after a lot of argument, they have gone, Noreen turns to me: 'Am I my brother's keeper?' She gives her clear, high laugh, the laugh of a young girl.

I say nothing, as I begin to lock and bolt the front door before we go to bed.

'What hypocrisy!' Noreen says.

Still I say nothing. I am thinking of that typescript of Bob's autobiography, a vial of poison on the point of exploding from the pressure building up within it, in the desk drawer behind us. I am thinking of it and the years in the Black Box.

What right have I to preach morality to anyone?

'They've upset you,' Noreen tells me, putting an arm round my shoulders. 'Why don't you have a night-cap before you turn in?'

'Let's both have a night-cap.'

'Oh, all right!' She giggles. 'How shocked Ivor and Claudine would be if they knew we were up to anything so wicked!'

17

After Mrs Pavlovsky had given me a key, I could go in and out of her house without ringing the bell. But for once I had forgotten it.

'Oh, it's you, Mervyn! Oh, I am glad! I thought of ringing you or your mama.' Although it was past ten o'clock, she was in dressing-gown and slippers trodden down at the heels, with her scant, grey hair screwed up in curlers. 'I'm sorry to be like this. But I'm getting ready for a wedding. My sister's second daughter. Come in, come in! Yes, I really am glad to see you, I really am.'

'Is something the matter?' Through the open door of the one room of the house which she occupied, I could hear a bath running. I had never before realised that she had a bathroom of her own.

'Just a mo.' She disappeared to turn off the water. 'That geyser's playing up,' she announced on her return. 'I had the gas-man in only last week. He told me I needed a new one, that this one was dangerous. But how am I to afford a new geyser?' She put a hand on my arm. Even then, at only seventeen, I could feel the pathos of that hand – the nails chipped and broken, the skin engrained with dirt – which constantly cleaned other people's houses when it was not cleaning her own. 'He's bad,' she said. 'Your father's really bad.'

'Ill?'

'Not physically.' She removed the hand and tapped her forehead. 'Here. I'm afraid he's got worse.'

'I'd better go and see.'

As I began to mount the bare, creaking treads of the stairs, she said: 'I hope I'm not to blame. That's what worries me. I asked him for the rent last Sunday and then again yesterday. Perhaps that got him down. But, as I told you, I need that money. I had to buy a present – a wedding present – for my niece. And I have to help my son and his wife . . .'

'I'm sure his condition has nothing to do with you. He's suffered from this neurasthenia ever since the War.' I seemed to hear Ma saying the word in answer to my question about what was wrong with Dad, so many years before, when we were returning home from Victoria Station in a taxi after seeing him off to Italy.

'I'd hate to be the cause of a relapse for him.'

'Don't worry about it!'

His door was ajar. He was sitting in the one armchair by the window, in nothing but a cotton vest and pants and a pair of socks, rucked about his ankles. His hair was tousled and there was a blueish-grey growth of hair on his chin and upper lip.

'Dad!'

His adam's apple bobbed up and down but no sound emerged. He stared at me with eyes so red that I wondered if he had been crying. I had often seen him cry before, on and on, as though from some inconsolable grief. I hated it when he did it. I hoped that he was not going to cry before me now.

'What's the problem?'

I saw the tray on the table beside him. There were some uneaten fingers of toast, congealed in their butter, a teacup full of tea, an apple. Although the rent was unpaid, good, kind Mrs Pavlovsky had clearly been attempting to feed him.

[92]

I pointed: 'Why haven't you had any of this?'

He shook his head. 'Can't.' The sound was so weak that I hardly heard it.

'But you must eat something. And drink something. You can't just starve yourself.'

I crossed over to him, bent down, put an arm round his shoulders. 'Dear Dad! Please! Try to eat something!'

He stared fixedly out of the window, his left leg twitching up and down. He might never have heard me. I felt bewildered, frightened, exasperated. He had often been monosyllabic during his depressions, but he had never before failed to make any response whatever to me. What on earth was going on? It was only years later, during my imprisonment in the Black Box, that I came to know the answer to that question.

I drew up the other, straight-backed chair and, knee to knee with him, took both his hands in mine. I experienced an extraordinary yearning tenderness, as of a mother for a stricken child. I massaged his hands.

Then, as though the massage had brought life back not merely into the hands but into his heart and his brain, he said: 'Your mother. Tell your mother I want to see her. Must see her. Tell her. Just for a few minutes.'

'Of course I'll tell her. I'm sure she'll come. We're leaving for Como on Monday but I'm sure she'll come. Don't worry.'

'Must see her,' he repeated. Then all at once he smiled: 'How is school going?'

'It's the holidays now. We broke up last week.'

'Holidays? How time flies!'

'Do you remember when you sang those Lieder for me? At school? In the car? You've never sung them for me again.'

[93]

'Never sung them again.' He repeated it. Then he fixed me with those raw eyes. 'What is the point?' he asked.

'What is the point of what?'

'Of the whole bloody business.'

Years later I was to understand the question; but now it merely added to my bewilderment and disquiet. 'How are you off for money? I met Mrs Pavlovsky in the hall and she said – '

'Owe rent. Can't pay it. What am I to do?'

'I'll speak to Ma.'

'No, no! Don't bother her.'

'Yes! I'll speak to her. Didn't your pension arrive this month?'

'Disappeared.'

'What do you mean?'

'Money arrived. Registered post. As per usual. Then disappeared.'

Had Mrs Pavlovsky taken it? Had one of the other tenants taken it? Or had Dad put it away somewhere and then forgotten it? 'But that's impossible. How could that be? I'll ask Mrs P. about it. She may know.'

'No, no! Don't ask her! Leave it!'

Eventually I went into the little kitchenette which he shared with two of the other tenants and made him some tea. Was the tea in the caddy his or did it belong to someone else? Oh, to hell with it! I'd use it, whoever was the owner. In a tin I found some crumbling shortbread biscuits. I'd give him some of those too.

Back in the room, I lifted the cup to his trembling lips, I inserted one piece of biscuit after another between his teeth. With difficulty he gulped; slowly he munched.

'That's better,' he said. I really believed that it – and he – were better.

[94]

From then on, I occasionally managed to get a few words out of him. But for most of the time I was just gazing at him and he was just gazing out of the window. Eventually I looked at my watch. Oh, heavens! I had persuaded Ma to take me to *Time and the Conways* that evening, even though she disliked Priestley, whom she repeatedly described at 'pretentious' or 'vulgar'. If I did not hurry, we should be late.

'Dad, I'm afraid I must leave you now. But I'll come by tomorrow. Or the day after tomorrow,' I amended, selfishly remembering that there were so many other things I wished to do before our departure for Como.

'Don't bother, don't bother.' His indifference was wounding. Then he went on: 'But your mother. Tell her. I want to see her. Must see her. Why does she never come to see me? Why?' So impassive before, he now spoke in anger. 'Why, why, why?'

'Ma, I really do think that you ought to go over.'

Ma, sprawled on the bed, continued to paint her toenails.

'Ma!'

'I heard you. There's no ought about it.'

'He's in a bad way. I've never seen him in a worse.'

'Then you're lucky. Pity is like money in the bank. If one keeps drawing on it, there's eventually none left. I'm afraid that's my situation now.'

'It would mean so much to him to have a visit from you.'

'Have you any idea, any idea at all, of how much I have to do before we leave? I simply cannot, cannot, spare the time. I'd like to, but that's the truth, I'm afraid.'

I sat glumly in the chair by her bed. Then I ventured:

[95]

'Well, if it's absolutely impossible for you to go there, do you think you could let me have some money to take him?'

'Money!' Brush in hand, she glared up at me. 'Are you crazy? Have you any idea of the money I've spent on him over all these years? Thousands, literally thousands!'

'But surely now that Aunt Bertha . . .'

'Don't please get it into your head that Aunt Bertha left me a fortune. She left me this house, she left me what's in it. But most of her money went to animals. You didn't get a penny and the pennies that came to me can almost be counted on the fingers of one hand.' She stared at me, brows knitted, in growing exasperation. 'You're just like your father. You have absolutely no sense of money at all. I don't know where you think it comes from. Your school fees are huge. To take you and your grubby little friend to Como is going to cost me a fortune. And Tim never pays his way, you know that. No, I'm sorry. Your father has his pension and he'll just have to learn to manage on that. What does he do with it, for God's sake?'

I had no answer to that question. I got up and wandered over to the window.

'Tim has arrived,' I said.

The new MG sports car, which I was convinced Ma must have given to him, was drawing up to the kerb.

'Oh, lord! Now you've made me late! We'll never get to the theatre on time.'

18

The next day I had decided what to do. Dad must have that money, and I must get it for him in the only way of which I could think.

At the back of a rosewood display cabinet in the drawing-room was a little gold French vinaigrette, with an Italian mosaic cover, probably Roman, of a spaniel. Aunt Bertha had once got it out and showed it to me, after I had bought a far less elegant and valuable one in nearby Church Street with money from a birthday. 'I bought it for the spaniel,' she told me. 'Isn't he a darling? I once had a spaniel exactly like that.'

I was sure that Mother had never noticed the vinaigrette; and even if she had, she was unlikely to miss it, so crammed was that display cabinet with knick-knacks, many of them of little artistic or financial value.

At the Caledonian Market, I knew an elderly Cockney stall-holder, a toff-like character with a huge belly and extremely thin legs, who wore a brown bowler hat, a brown cashmere overcoat with a velveteen collar, and rings on almost all of his purple, stubby fingers. I liked him and he seemed to like me, since he would almost always sell me things for much less than their first quoted price. Another stall-holder, a scrawny woman in a hair-net and tippet, had warned me that he was 'a terrible old rogue – half the stuff he sells has been nicked'; but that did not worry me.

He turned the vinaigrette over and over in those swollen, purple, heavily beringed hands. I could see that he was literally salivating. As with me, so with him the appetite for something beautiful and rare was almost physical. 'Very jolly,' he fluted in his parody of an upper-class voice, 'très, très jolly indeed. How much were you thinking of asking for it, squire?'

'Well, what do you think of offering?' I had yet to learn the art of bargaining.

He named a ridiculously low sum and half-heartedly I raised it. His eyebrows shot up, he whistled. 'Cor!' He had momentarily forgotten to be the toff. Then he said: 'Tell you what, squire. I'll meet you half-way. How's that for generosity?'

Foolishly I accepted.

I turned the key in the front door and I knew at once, as one so often knows, that the whole house was empty. Even then, I had a feeling of doom. 'Mrs Pavlovsky!' I called, planning to give her the rent. Then I knocked on her door. 'Mrs Pavlovsky!' Ah, well, she must be out; and probably at that hour, just before noon, all her lodgers were also out.

I began to mount the stairs, growing increasingly breathless as I did so. At the landing outside Dad's room I paused and placed a hand in my trouser pocket. Yes, the grubby, tattered notes were there. I would tell Dad that they were from Ma. After all, in a sense they were, since it was she, not I, who had inherited the vinaigrette from Aunt Bertha; and it would make him happy to think that she had been generous to him, even if she had not been able to find the time for a visit.

I pushed open the door.

The first thing that I noticed was a sock rumpled around an ankle. Then I looked upwards to the hide-

usly swollen face above the noose of the Coldstream
e.

The bulging eyes looked even redder than on my
revious visit.

19

r Unwin carefully adjusted the blotter on his desk. He
ad, I had long since observed, a passion for symmetry.
'And did you feel any guilt?'
'For stealing the vinaigrette? No, none at all. She
wed him that. And much more,' I added.
'No, I didn't mean the vinaigrette. I meant his death.'
'I wasn't responsible for his death. Why should I
ave felt guilty about it?'
He did not answer.
'I did all I could for him. I visited him as often as I
ould.'
'And your mother? Did she feel any guilt?'
Did she? I pondered it. No. At first she seemed
tally callous, horrifying me by her angry: 'Oh, God!'
hen given the news, followed by her: 'He *would*
oose the time when we're just about to leave for
omo. Totally thoughtless to the last.' But then, late
at night, I had heard her sobbing in the bedroom next
mine. I had wondered whether to go in to comfort
er. Then I had thought: 'No. Let her bloody well stew
her own juice.'
'Did your mother feel any guilt?' Dr Unwin repeated.
had been absent from his room for some time, lost in

thought, even though my body had been seated acros
the desk from him.

'I don't think so. No. I think she felt grief,' I addec
'Surprisingly. Her love for him seemed to have die
such a long time before.'

'Perhaps she was grieving for what he had bee
when they first met and married and fell in love?'

'Possibly. Yes.'

'What did you feel about her? After it had happenec
I mean?'

I stared at him. 'I don't know,' I eventually answerec
Nor did I.

But he didn't believe me. 'Oh, come on! You mu
have blamed her, didn't you?'

I didn't want to think about it. I didn't want t
answer.

'After all, if she had visited him and paid the re
and given him an allowance – well, perhaps he wou
never have done what he did?'

'Perhaps.'

'In a way, she murdered him. Or, at least, was th
cause of his death?'

Was it really Dr Unwin who put those questions t
me? Or did I put them to myself, as I sat, totally silen
in 'my' armchair by the window?

It is odd that I do not remember. I really do n
remember. I really do not know.

s Ma kept saying, Dad's death 'really couldn't have
me at a more inconvenient time.' We had to postpone
ir journey to Como, our cook and maid had to
stpone their visits to their families, and Bob had to
end another week at the Bexhill holiday home.
ouldn't Bob stay with us in London? I pleaded with
a. I knew how much he hated that home. But she
as adamant. 'I have far too much to think about
ithout him on my hands,' she told me emphatically.

There was an inquest, at which the coroner reached
e predictable verdict that Dad had killed himself
hile the balance of his mind was disturbed'. He
anted to make it clear that no blame attached to
nyone; the deceased was one of those unfortunate
en who had never fully recovered from his experi-
ces in the War.

The funeral was out at Putney Vale, to which Tim
rove Ma and me in the new MG but which he declined
attend himself – 'Oh, God, no! I'll go and look up
ie of my buddies who lives not far from here.' There
ere some half-dozen fellow officers of Dad's and their
ives, the charwoman who had cleaned for us in the
ys when we lived in Prince of Wales Drive (how, I
ondered, had she, obviously not a *Times* reader, come
hear of the death?), and Mrs Pavlovsky, who arrived
eathless and flustered half-way through the service,
utching a bunch of flowers which scattered their
tals as she hurried down the aisle.

Suddenly Ma began once again to cry, raising th
black net veil of the pill-box hat which she had worn f
Founder's Day at Gladbury and then pressing a wad o
handkerchief first to one eye and then the other. I felt
sudden impulse of tenderness for her and placed m
hand over the hand not holding the handkerchief. The
I thought: Oh, this is all just theatre! She's crying lik
that because widows are supposed to cry at funerals.
wanted to hiss at her: Do stop it! You're taking no or
in.

Behind me I could hear someone else crying, no
discreetly like Ma, but in windy gulps and gasps.
turned round. It was Mrs Pavlovsky, her wide fac
cracking apart with what I was sure was genuine gri
under that scarf which, outdoors and in, she almo
always wore over her head.

'Are you going to have some sort of binge afte
wards?' Tim had asked Ma, for her to reply: 'Certain'
not! I hate that idea of everyone forgetting all about th
dead person in order to swill and guzzle.' What sh
really hated, I was sure, was the idea of having f
entertain a number of dull people (as she would se
them) scarcely known to her.

In consequence, after we had left the chapel, peop
hung around for a short, awkward time, in the expe
tation of some kind of invitation and then, realisir
that none would be forthcoming, wandered of
Eventually only Mrs Pavlovsky remained, bending ov
the few bouquets and wreaths in order to decipher th
messages and names among them. Her own bunch c
wilting flowers was also lying there.

Having completed this task, she straightened u
looked around her, and then hurried over to m
'Mervyn! Dear Mervyn!' Suddenly her arms we
around me, her lips were on my cheek. 'It is so sac

sad! I feel deeply for you, Mervyn! You were a good son, good, good, good!' Although she had met Ma, she said nothing whatever to her. She even avoided looking at her.

Tim now at our side, we watched Mrs Pavlovsky trudging up the path from the chapel to the main road. Then I said: 'Couldn't we give her a lift? It's such a long way to the station and there aren't many buses.'

'Certainly not!' Ma replied, no doubt bruised by Mrs Pavlovsky's refusal to acknowledge her. 'I could never stand that woman. Always so greedy for money. And so insincere. She didn't really care a damn about your father. All she wanted was that rent – which was far too high for that scruffy neighbourhood.'

Tim took up: 'Anyway she'd never have been able to fit herself into the back of the old MG. It would be like trying to squeeze an elephant into a rabbit hutch.'

Ma's laughter rang out across the now deserted cemetery. 'Oh, Tim, you do have a wonderful way with words! You should have been a writer, not an actor.'

'Now I've got an idea,' Tim said. 'How about my driving us down to the Waldorf for tea? Mervyn can eat loads and loads of scones and sandwiches and cakes, and you and I can dance.'

'Lovely!' Ma exclaimed.

21

Before we left for Italy, Bob spent the night with us.

I had suggested to Ma that perhaps Tim could drive over to Victoria Station to meet him off the Bexhill train,

[103]

but she had said: 'Don't be silly! He's far too busy. Surely your friend can find his own way here? He's not a child after all.'

I almost asked what it was that Tim was doing that made him so busy. But I knew that such a question would only upset her. Since he had come to live with us, he had done no work at all, other than unsuccessfully attending an audition for a Cochran review and another for an Ivor Novello musical.

From the farthest end of the long platform I glimpsed Bob striding out towards the ticket barrier. Even before he himself saw me, he looked extraordinarily eager and happy. He was wearing a Harris tweed jacket over an open-necked shirt, flared grey flannel trousers pinched in at the waist by a snake-belt, gymshoes and a battered trilby hat tipped rakishly over an eyebrow. In one hand was a large suitcase, with a rope knotted around it, and in the other a canvas bag. What would Ma say about his appearance?

Catching sight of me, he dropped both suitcase and bag and sprinted towards me. 'Mervyn!' By now, we called each other by our Christian names when not at Gladbury. He gripped my arm while at the same time shaking my hand. 'Terrific!' I knew then that, whereas I was dreading the Como holiday, he was overjoyed by the prospect of it.

We sat opposite to each other on the 52 bus, talking loudly across its gangway. Passengers scowled at us but neither of us cared. For days now I had been feeling isolated; Ma was so much taken up with Tim that she rarely paid any attention to me; Tim himself, though friendly enough, treated me like a child. Now at last I had a companion. As always, this companion could make me feel far cleverer, far more amusing and far more observant than I ever felt without him.

'I'm sorry about your father,' Bob eventually said. 'I only met him that once, at Founder's Day. But he seemed a decent sort of bloke.'

'Yes,' I said. 'Thank you.' I was embarrassed, as I was always embarrassed when anyone commiserated with me about Dad's death.

'Why did he do it?'

'Let's talk about it when we've got off the bus.' I had become aware that a woman on the seat beside him was listening to us avidly.

'Okay.'

As we trudged along the Bayswater Road, I now carrying the canvas bag for him, he repeated his question: 'What made him do such a thing?'

'He was pretty unhappy. The War. He couldn't get over it. And then . . . my mother . . .' I broke off. I did not wish to be disloyal to her, however bitter my thoughts.

'What had she to do with it?'

'Well . . .' I hesitated. Then the pressure was too strong. I began to tell him about Ma's lovers – or, rather, 'boyfriends', as she and therefore I always called them; about her expelling Dad from the house; about her refusal to give him money; about her refusal to visit him.

To my amazement, he then said: 'I wonder if you're not being a little too hard on her.'

'What do you mean?'

'Well, you ought to try to see things from her point of view too. All those years of being married to him couldn't have been much fun. Could they?'

'No . . . I suppose not . . .'

'It's terribly difficult to live with a neurotic. Everyone knows that. Your mother's so full of fun, so she'd feel particularly badly – I mean, the long silences, the depressions, the refusal to do anything.' He turned his head and peered up into my face. 'Yes, you really must look at things from her point of view as well.'

We had entered into the square and were nearing the house.

'Do you live here? In this square?'

'Yes. That's our house.' I pointed.

'That? But it's huge!'

'Yes, it is pretty big.'

His awe delighted me.

When I came down to dinner, I at once noticed the polo-neck sweater. It was of light blue silk and, with the money which I had intended for Dad, I had bought it the day before in the Burlington Arcade. Tim was wearing it.

He laughed, a glass of dry martini in his hand, when he saw me staring at it. Then he said: 'I hope you don' mind?' I did not answer. 'Do you?'

'I've never worn it,' I said. 'It's brand new.'

'Oh, gosh! Have I put up a black? Bella said you wouldn't mind. I was passing your bedroom and the door was open and there it was lying across the bed. It goes perfectly with these fawn trousers and jacket. They're brand new too. Bella gave them to me.'

'You should have asked me first.'

'Oh, Mervyn, don't be such a bore! It's only a sweater. Tim's not going to harm it, now is he?'

'He should have asked me,' I repeated

'Sorry, old boy. Do you want me to take it off?' I did not reply. 'Do you?'

'No, of course he doesn't,' Ma said. 'It's just that he's in a bad mood. He gets these bad moods – just like his father.'

[106]

'Well, Mervyn, let me pour you a dry martini in expiation.' He picked up the cocktail shaker. 'I make dry martinis better than anyone else this side of the Atlantic. An American friend taught me how to make them.' Carefully he began to shave a piece off a lemon with the small, sharp knife which he always used for this purpose. Ma had specially bought it for him.

Was this the American of whom Ma had been so jealous? I looked over to her to see her reaction; but, lighting a cigarette, she had ceased to take any interest in our conversation.

'I'm not supposed to drink,' I said sulkily.

'Aren't you? Oh, dear! I used to drink gin with my mother's milk. . . . Bella – Mervyn can have a cocktail, can't he? It is the hols, after all.'

'Oh, give him what he wants,' Ma said in a cross voice. She dragged at her cigarette in its long amber holder. Then she asked. 'Where's your little friend?'

'Having a bath, I think.'

'About time too. He's terribly grubby. Smelly, as well. When I went into his room to get something from the chest of drawers, the stink was awful. And there were all these filthy clothes lying about, some on a chair but most on the floor. Does he expect Isabel to wash them for him here? Or does he expect the maid at the villa to wash them? Isabel wouldn't have the time. The maid at the villa may well give notice when faced with such a job.'

I often told Bob that he was dirty, that he stank, that he really should have a bath and change his clothes. But it was one thing for me to say these things, another for her to do so. I scowled at her in fury.

Tim handed me a misted glass. 'That'll put you in a better mood,' he said. 'Mark my words.'

At last Bob appeared. His hair, still wet from his

bath, was sleeked down, and he was wearing a suit, the arms and legs of which were far too long for him. In his right hand he was carrying something in a paper bag.

He went over to Ma. 'Mrs Frost, I brought you a little present.' He held out the bag.

'Oh, Bob, how sweet of you! What is it?'

From the paper bag she drew out a half-pound box of milk chocolates. She turned it over, squinting down. 'Oh, what a surprise! How did you know that I just love milk chocolates? This *is* a treat!'

Bob grinned with pleasure.

Ma's sarcasm was totally lost on him.

22

Ma was happy, as she went from room to room and then, throwing open the french windows, walked out on to the terrace with its shimmering view of the lake. Tim, Bob and I were following after her.

'Wonderful! It's even better than I had hoped.'

'It ought to be wonderful at that extortionate price,' Tim said.

He had already complained that the car, left by the owners for us to use, was 'a museum piece', and that his bedroom, next to Ma's, overlooked not the lake but the main road – 'You know I'm a terrible insomniac.'

About the bedroom Bob had at once volunteered: 'I don't mind changing with you. I sleep like a top.'

But Ma had not in the least cared for this idea. Bob's

and my bedrooms were on the top floor, above hers and Tim's, and of course she wanted Tim to be next to her. 'No, no!' she had snapped fretfully. 'Let's leave things as they are. In any case, in a place like this, I'm sure there's virtually no traffic at night.'

Now Tim peered down at the motor boat chugging across from the next little town to the landing stage of the one, Bellagio, in which we were staying. 'That boat's terribly slow,' he said.

'Does that matter?' Ma asked. 'We're unlikely to want to go anywhere in a hurry. Oh, Tim, do stop finding fault with everything.' I had heard her and him bickering in their shared first-class sleeper, and now they were at it again.

'The water looks so inviting,' Tim went on. 'But it's probably fearfully cold. Do you think one can swim in it?'

'If it is too cold, the Serbelloni has a pool,' Ma retorted even more crossly.

'Bob can't swim,' I announced.

'You can't swim!' Ma turned towards him. 'I've never heard of such a thing. A boy of your age!'

Bob grinned, not all upset by the revelation. 'Everyone at Gladbury is supposed to be able to swim. But I just sink like a stone.'

'I'll teach you,' Tim said. 'Tomorrow. In the pool or in the lake, whichever is warmer.' Ever since our arrival, he had been going out of his way to be friendly and helpful to us.

'No thanks! I loathe water.'

'Is that why you wash so little?' Ma asked, making it sound like a joke, although I knew it to be a jibe.

Bob laughed. 'Yes. I suppose so. I also loathe soap.'

'Well, I'm hungry,' Ma said. 'Let's see what Maria has prepared for us.'

Maria and her daughter, Violetta, had come with the house.

That afternoon Ma was lying out on the terrace in a bathing costume unusually skimpy for that period. She was avidly reading *The Constant Nymph*, the author of which, Margaret Kennedy, she had once or twice met as a neighbour. 'One wouldn't have thought that a woman like that could have written anything so racy,' she told us.

Bob came into my bedroom, where I was loading my Box Brownie, and peered out of the window. Then he exclaimed: 'Gosh!'

'What is it?'

'Come and take a dekko at this!'

Ma had rolled down the upper part of her bathing costume, to reveal her surprisingly large and firm breasts.

Bob, elbows resting on window sill and chin resting on hands, stared downwards. 'They're super! Just look at them! You'd never think she was a day over twenty.'

I glanced down, then turned away and returned to my camera. I was not merely embarrassed to look any longer; I was also panicky.

'Oh, Christ. I'm getting a hard on!'

'Get away from there! Bob! *Bob!*' I strode over, caught him by an arm, and tugged him away.

'Hang on a mo!'

'No! Just behave yourself!'

'What am I to do about this?' He pointed to his erection, all at once reminding me of that time when he had masturbated before me.

'I've no idea. I'm certainly not going to do anything about it.'

[110]

'Oh, come on!'

Was he joking or was he serious?

'Let's get going!' I said crossly. We had hired bicycles and were planning, over-ambitiously, to circle the lake.

'Let me have just one more peek!'

'No!'

I bundled him through the door.

Violetta could not have been more than fifteen or sixteen. Her cheeks were round and red and there was a deep dimple in her chin. A plait of thick black hair fell over a shoulder, and there was a faint shadow of hair along her upper lip. Her breasts were firm and large and her bare legs muscular, no doubt from the long walk up from the village to the villa high up on its spur of a hill. During lunch and then again during dinner I had been aware of Tim constantly, if furtively, examining her. I was sure that Ma was aware of it too.

After dinner Ma said: 'You'd think they'd have taught that girl to wait properly at table. She just thrusts the food at one. And she kept appearing on the wrong side.'

'What is the right side?' Bob asked.

Ma ignored him. 'When I tried to talk to her, she seemed to be half-witted,' she went on.

'Perhaps she was confused by your Italian,' Tim said.

'My Italian is perfectly adequate. No Italian ever has any difficulty in understanding it.'

'I meant, darling, that perhaps she speaks some dialect. Your Italian is *lingua toscana in bocca Romana.* Which is as it should be.' He was clearly mocking her. He had already told us that his own Italian had been learned as a boy, when his parents had taken up

[111]

residence in Alassio because the cost of living was so much lower in Italy than in England.

Ma sighed. 'If only one of these louts could play bridge, we could have a rubber together.'

'We could teach them,' Tim suggested.

Surprisingly Ma welcomed the suggestion. 'Oh, all right. Do go upstairs and fetch the cards, Mervyn. They're on my dressing-table.'

I was a hopeless pupil, Bob a brilliant one. As an adult, he was often to play championship bridge.

'I can see that you're much brighter than my poor son,' Ma told him.

'Of course he is,' I agreed. 'He's already in the sixth and I'm still stuck in the remove.'

'Well, your father never had much brain, either.'

His bathing things in a rolled-up towel under an arm, Tim was talking to Violetta in the hall. From the sitting-room I could hear them. So could Ma, who was writing some postcards on her knee, with a large, old-fashioned rolled-gold fountain pen, once Aunt Bertha's. Head on one side and tip of tongue protruding from between her glistening, scarlet lips, she listened for a while. Then she jumped to her feet and strode to the door. 'Violetta!' I heard her call. 'Violetta!' There followed a stream of no doubt inaccurate and mispronounced Italian, intermittently interrupted by Violetta's frightened '*Scusi, signora, scusi!*'

Then Tim was saying in a bored, languid voice 'Oh, Bella sweetie, don't, please don't, be such a bore!'

'Would you mind! I'm talking to the girl, not you. This house has to be cleaned and now is the time when she ought to be cleaning it. *Now!*'

Bob sneaked into the room. 'They're having a terrific row,' he whispered.

'Just an argument,' I corrected. 'I think they really enjoy them.'

'She's jealous.'

'Rubbish!'

But of course he was right.

Having bicycled a considerable way round the lake in one direction on the previous day, we now set off in the opposite one. We pedalled lazily, zigzagging from side to side, since there was virtually no traffic, while talking to each other.

'What do you suppose they do, actually do?'

'Oh, shut up!'

'I mean, do you think The One and Only fucks her? He looks as if he must be a queer. But she wouldn't want to go around all the time with a queer, would she? And if he were a queer, he wouldn't be so interested in Violetta.'

I shot ahead of him, bicycling hard. I hated the subject, I was frightened of it.

'I wish she'd get interested in me.' He had overtaken me.

'Some hope! You're far too young. And ugly. And smelly.'

He laughed, not in the least offended. 'She seems to like them young.'

Eventually we halted so that I could have a swim. Bob got into bathing trunks but refused to enter the lake with me. Instead, he sat out on the bank, arms crossed and feet dangling in the water.

I soon emerged, shuddering. 'Golly, it's cold! Freezing!'

'It's all that water coming down from the Alps.'

Briskly I began to rub myself down with a towel, while Bob began to dress.

'While you were in there,' he told me, while pulling his vest over his head, 'I was thinking of colour blindness. Did you realise that Tim is colour blind? Your mother asked him for one of those sweets; she said: "Give me the green one," and he hadn't a clue which one to give her. It's odd, you know, colour blindness is found more often in men than in women. The reason is that a father transmits his X-chromosomes to all his daughters but to none of his sons, whereas a mother passes one of her two X's to each of her children. Did you know that?'

I shook my head, uninterested.

'Genetics are fascinating,' he said. 'I really want to learn German so that I can read Mendel's paper in the original. He was an amazing man.'

'Yes, you've told me all about him.' I almost added: Often.

Dressed, Bob pointed: 'Look at all those roses! Have you ever seen roses like that?'

Beside us, there was a low wall and, beyond it, a large, modern villa. In front of the villa there was a formal garden, scrupulously weeded, with beds of hybrid roses, such as Ma would never allow in the Campden Hill Square garden, finding them 'vulgar' or 'common' – two favourite epithets of hers.

'I'm going to pick some,' he said.

'You can't. It's a private garden.' Just as he was naturally lawless, I was naturally law-abiding. 'Bob!'

He had begun to climb the wall. As he did so, I heard the frenzied barking of a dog.

As soon as he had jumped down on the other side, an Alsatian, head lowered and coat bristling, rushed up. I watched in horror, certain that the dog would maul him. With his usual fearlessness, Bob stooped, lowered a hand, made encouraging noises. In a moment, the dog had slunk up to him and had begun to lick his fingers.

Followed by the dog, Bob walked over to one of the rose bushes. He struggled to break off a branch and eventually succeeded in doing so. He approached another bush and, tugging at it, swore 'Fuck!' as he scratched a thumb. Eventually he clambered back over the wall, a huge bouquet gripped in a hand.

'I thought you were going to be torn apart.'

He sucked at the scratch. 'Dogs are like humans. You must never show them you're frightened.'

Having tied the roses on to the carrier of the bicycle, he jumped astride it. 'These roses are for someone very special,' he said.

I did not need to ask him who the someone very special was.

Ma examined the roses. 'Oh, how kind of you, Bob,' she said in a perfunctory voice. 'Where did you get these?'

'An old woman was selling them by the roadside,' he lied.

Ma again examined them. She wrinkled up her small, retroussé nose. 'I hope you didn't pay too much,' she said. 'They're really rather past it.' She gave the bunch a shake. Like the bouquet brought by Mrs Pavlovsky to Dad's funeral, this one at once shed some petals. 'You can always rely on an Italian to do you down,' Ma said.

*

The next morning, Bob asked me: 'Where do you think she put the flowers?'

'What flowers?'

'The roses, idiot! I can't see them anywhere.'

'Perhaps they're in her bedroom.'

He shrugged, unconvinced.

That afternoon we were exploring the large, overgrown garden, which fell down, in a series of crumbling terraces, to the lake. There was a small wooden summer-house, which could be rotated on an axle to catch the sun. There were also chicken hutches and a chicken run, enclosed with wire netting, but no chickens; an asparagus bed, in which the asparagus was as tall as the cow-parsley around it; and a rusty incinerator, from which acrid smoke was mounting in lethargic coils.

Bob peered into the incinerator. Then he coughed, as the smoke crept into his lungs, and cried out: 'Take a look at this!'

I went over. On top of a smouldering mound of vegetable peelings, old newspapers and wrapping paper, some roses were scattered, their petals shrivelled and brown, their stems black.

'My roses,' he said.

'Are they? They must be some other ones,' I said, although I knew that they were his.

Again he leaned over the incinerator and again he coughed from the smoke.

'Why do you think she threw them away? Why?' He turned and faced me. 'Your fucking mother threw them away!'

It was from that time that I noticed a total change in

his attitude to Ma. He had loved her. Now he hated her.

The abruptness of this change, as though a once brilliantly lit room had, at the touch of a switch, been plunged into darkness, has never ceased to puzzle me. In my own case, the transition from love to loathing was infinitely slow, paralleling the medical history of a neighbour of ours who died a month or two ago. Over the years, even though he continued successfully with his job as a dentist, this man's behaviour became more and more erratic. Now he seemed to be in a state of vegetable torpor, now in one of feverish excitement. Then, after some kind of seizure in the high street, he was discovered to have a brain tumour. Apparently he had had it for ten or eleven years. The hatred within me grew with a similar slowness. But Bob succumbed to his hatred with the devastating speed with which, in a tropical country, a man totally healthy one day has expired by the next.

23

We had hired a boat. I was rowing, since Bob was so clumsy at doing so, and he was lolling at the other end, the strings of the rudder in his hands.

'What's your mother doing?' he asked.

'She said she was going to have a siesta.'

'She's still got a hangover.'

'No, she hasn't. Don't talk bilge.'

'All that drinking last night. First the row, then the drinking.'

'That wasn't a row. That was just an argument.'

'If you ask me, he's not fucking her enough. Women get like that when they're not being fucked as much as they want.'

'Oh, shut up!'

'It's well known. And a woman as highly sexed as your mother . . . That's probably the main reason why she gave your father the push.'

Scowling, as I panted at the oars, I said nothing. Perhaps, probably, what he was saying was true. But, as so often when he had some criticism of Ma, I did not want him to put it into words, I did not want to hear it.

Suddenly I was aware of the din of a motor boat approaching.

'Look out!' Bob warned.

As the motor boat roared past, our little craft rocked frantically from side to side. What would happen if it capsized? Since Bob could not swim, he would probably drown.

'Shits!' I muttered.

Then Bob said: 'Golly! Do you know who was on board?'

I rested the oars. 'Who?'

'Tim. And he was wearing your sweater again. And he was with that American who's staying at the Serbelloni.'

'Which American?'

'The one Tim talked to by the pool. Don't you remember? You must remember. You thought he must be a pansy.'

On that previous occasion, the elderly American had been wearing a white, short-sleeved shirt, white shorts which revealed legs on which the varicose veins stood out like knotted red and purple cords, and huge sunglasses which covered more than half his face. He had sat in a deck-chair reading the *New York Herald Tribune*. From time to time he had lowered this newspaper in order to stare at me, while I lay sunbathing not far from him and Tim was trying to teach Bob to swim. Later, he and Tim had gone into the hotel bar for a drink, leaving Bob and me by the pool. Later still, on the way home, Tim had told us airily that the American was 'someone involved in show business', whom he had met at a London party.

'What's going on?' Bob asked.

'What do you mean?'

'Why should The One and Only be with him? He said he was going into Como to do some shopping. Remember? He was going to take the vaporetto.'

'Perhaps he missed it.'

'Then he could have taken the next. They go every twenty minutes . . . What do you know about Tim?'

'Very little. Dad called him a chorus-boy.'

'A gigolo more likely. Your mother's batty to waste so much money on him.'

That evening Tim eyed us warily. No doubt he was fearful that we would betray to Ma, either deliberately or accidentally, that we had seen him in the motor boat with the American.

'Are the shops in Como any good?' Ma asked, removing the dark glasses which she had obviously been wearing because of her hangover.

Tim shook his head. 'Not really.'

'Did you buy anything?'

'I almost bought a tie. But it was ridiculously expensive. I could buy one like it for half the price at Sulka's. And I almost bought you a bag,' he added. 'Rather attractive. But again . . . I'll buy you one in London instead.'

[119]

Ma smiled at him and then impulsively put out a hand to his cheek. 'You're so good to me!'

'And you're so good to me!' He took the hand and pulled it to his chest.

It amazed me that he should be able to lie with such facility.

24

I have just left Noreen at the Royal Sussex, where she is to have the first of a series of gold injections.

'It sounds terribly extravagant,' she told me as, with a grimace of pain, she settled herself into the seat beside me in the car and fastened the safety belt.

'Don't worry. You're worth your weight in gold.'

She liked my silly joke. 'In lead more likely,' she said. 'I get so tired of heaving this ancient carcass around.'

'Now don't talk like that!'

We both laughed.

Now I am in the reference room of the public library, turning over the pages of Who's Who. Of course Bob will be in it, whereas I should qualify only for a volume of Who's Nobody. Ah, here he is! The knighthood. The foreign orders. The membership of innumerable committees and societies. The professorship in England and the subsequent one in the States. Yes, the entry gives a private address. I was afraid that, like many eminent people, he might withhold it. I write it down. It is not all that far away, in a village the other side of Canterbury. I could drive there easily.

Back in the car, I wonder yet again why he should

have sent me the typescript and enclosed no covering letter or even an address with it. Was he trying to punish me? Or taunt me? Or provoke me? Or challenge me?

As always, I cannot be sure of his motives.

25

As Bob and I walked up from one crumbling, over-grown terrace to another, we heard the angry voices. What would the two elderly women in the next-door villa be thinking? They spent most of the day at their needlework out on their terrace. Each had a sallow, lined face, and grey hair pulled back into a small, tight bun. Each hobbled on a stick. Tim thought that they were twins, but Ma, pointing out that one was taller than the other and had a bigger nose, was sure that they were 'girlfriends'. When they saw Bob and me over the low wall, they would always call out a greeting in Italian, their voices strident and hoarse.

We halted on the terrace. 'What's going on?' Bob asked. Already, from far off, we had heard Ma accuse Tim of being 'disloyal, utterly disloyal' and, a few seconds later, of being 'a bloody liar'. What Tim had replied to these accusations we had been unable to hear.

Now Ma was saying: 'The first time you said you'd been to Como, I believed you. I always believe people, that's my nature, to believe and trust people. But when you said you were going over there to get the English Sundays and then came back empty-handed, saying you couldn't find any, well, that was when I began to wonder. And then I saw that English woman – the one who works in the Bank of England – at that coffee place and she was reading the *Sunday Times*. So I asked her where she had bought it. And do you know what she answered?' There was a pause; Tim must have made some reply, inaudible to us. '"In Como. This morning." That's what she answered. And then I asked her if they had all the Sundays and she said, Oh, yes, they had heaps and heaps of them – heaps and heaps of them, those were her words – even the *News of the World*.' A silence followed. Then Ma demanded: 'Well, what have you got to say to all that?'

I tugged at Bob's arm. But, jerking away, he refused to budge.

In a calm voice, Tim was replying: 'It's a fair cop. That's what I have to say. It's a fair cop. But if I've lied to you, it's because you make me lie to you.'

'*I* make you lie to me! What the fuck do you mean?'

'By this absurd possessiveness of yours. I daren't tell you I've gone out to meet a friend because then you immediately jump to conclusions.'

'And who was the friend you went out to meet when you were supposed to be getting the Sundays?'

'Do you really want to know?'

'Of course I want to know.'

'Well, if you must know, it was Aaron Platz.'

'What!' Ma screeched the word. 'Aaron Platz? What the hell is he doing here? Did he follow you?'

'He was coming to Italy in any case. Something to do with some co-production. So when I told him we should be here in Bellagio, he thought he might come here too for a few days of rest.'

'I bet he did! And you thought it might be fun for

[122]

you to have that old queen's company when you got bored with mine.'

Tim remained calm. 'Bella dear, your company is far more amusing than Aaron's. He bores me rigid. But one has to face the fact that he can do far more for my career than you can. I've always wanted to break into films, really break into them, instead of merely being an extra. He thinks I've got the right looks.'

Ma gave a jeering laugh. 'I bet he does! I just bet he does! He thinks you've got the right looks and the right cock and the right bum!'

Bob clapped a hand over his mouth, to staunch his laughter.

'Oh, for God's sake!' Now Tim too was angry; his voice had risen in both volume and pitch. 'There's nothing like that in our relationship. You should know that by now!'

'Oh, you'd be prepared to swing any way if it suited you. I'm afraid one just has to face it. You're always on the make.'

'It's all very well for you to talk in that superior way. You've never had to fight for anything in your whole bloody life. You've no idea what it's like to have been born with nothing, literally nothing, and to have had to struggle every inch of the way.' Now self-pity was leaking, an ever-widening stain, into his voice. 'You've always had it easy, bloody easy!'

Again I tugged at Bob's arm. I whispered: 'Let's go. Come on, let's go.'

But he shook his head, once more refusing to move.

'Oh, why do we have to quarrel like this, always quarrel like this?' Ma was suddenly wailing.

'Because you're so possessive and jealous, that's why! Because you're bloody impossible!'

[123]

Suddenly, we heard the crash of what I took to be a plate or a vase. In the past, Ma had hurled things at Dad, in sudden frenzies of rage. 'Fuck you, fuck you!' she was screaming.

Bob, no longer able to contain himself, guffawed. Then, fearing that he might have been heard, the two of us hurried away, round the side of the house.

'God! What a scene! I've never heard a scene like that,' he said to me as we entered the house through the kitchen door.

'Well, I have. Often.'

As so often after Ma and Tim had had a quarrel, they were literally inseparable. Arms linked, they swayed into dinner ahead of us. During dinner they were constantly touching each other, he putting a hand to her cheek, she putting a hand to his shoulder, one feeding the other with some titbit. Dinner over, they sprawled on the same sofa, she all but on top of him.

Eventually they announced that they were driving over to Como, to go to a night-club of which they had heard.

'May we come too?' I asked. I had never been to a night-club.

'Certainly not! You're far too young. You can both go to bed.'

For a while, Ma and Tim having left, Bob and I played chess. But bored with the ease with which he could defeat me – one game lasted little more than five minutes – Bob eventually pushed the board over, scattering the pieces across the marble floor.

'What did you do that for?'

'Oh, I can't be bothered to play with a nitwit like you. You learn nothing, you remember nothing.' He said it in so good-natured a way that I could not be upset.

'It's strange how quarrelling can arouse people sexually,' Bob went on. 'I'm sure they had a good fuck before dinner, after she'd screamed at him and thrown that vase at him. And when they get back from Como, I'm sure they'll have another good fuck.'

I was now on my hands and knees, picking up the scattered pieces.

'I shouldn't say this, I suppose, seeing that she's your mother. But she really is a terrible woman, isn't she?'

'Certainly not!'

But for the first time I realised that he was right. She was a terrible woman. It was only the pathos of her that had for so long disguised it from me.

'She caused your father's death. Yes? As good as.'

'Rubbish!'

But was it rubbish? I was doubtful.

'Only a little while ago you were telling me how wonderful she was,' I reminded him. 'You even stole some roses to give to her.'

Legs stuck out from the sofa on which he was reclining and hands deep in pockets, Bob scowled out through the french windows at the rapidly darkening sky. 'I know. The trouble is that she's so bloody attractive. Half the time I want to fuck her and half the time I want to kill her.' He laughed. 'Have you ever wanted to do either of those things?'

'Of course not! Don't be such an idiot!'

There would be a storm, I was sure, with one of those spectacular exhibitions of lightning, forking around the lake, which so much delighted Bob and me and so

[125]

much terrified Ma. It had become so oppressive that I was lying out on top of my bed in only my pyjama trousers, reading a copy of *Apollo* bought at Victoria Station on our way out. Even after all these years I can remember that I was reading an article about Britannia ware, of which I then knew little.

The door opened and there was Bob. He was wearing only a grubby pair of boxer shorts. He had, I had discovered, only one pair of pyjamas with him and they, along with the dirty laundry which he had brought with him from Bexhill, were being washed. 'I hope he's going to give Violetta a good tip at the end of this stay,' Ma had commented, and I had then replied: 'Oh, Ma, he's got hardly any money at all. His parents keep him terribly short.'

I wasn't pleased to see him. I wanted to forget what he had said about Ma. I wanted to hear nothing more from him about her.

'There's going to be a storm,' he said. 'I can't sleep. I was wondering whether to steal one of your mother's sleeping tablets.'

How did he know that Ma had sleeping tablets? She had never spoken of them in his presence, as far as I could remember. 'Have you ever been in her room?'

He laughed impudently. 'Not when she was there.'

'But at some other time?' I was indignant.

'Oh, don't take that high and mighty, holier-than-thou line! You've never been infatuated with anyone, you're far too cold and immature. But if you had been, then you'd know that, at such times, one wants to know everything, absolutely everything about the other person.' He threw himself down on to my bed, so that we were facing each other, his head at one end, mine at the other. 'I had a quick look at that medicine chest of hers. Those slimming pills are said to be dangerous.

She really shouldn't take them. People say they contain tape-worm eggs.'

'Oh, bilge! All they contain is dexedrine. Ma told me.' In those days it was possible to buy dexedrine over a chemist's counter.

'Anyway . . .' He closed his eyes. 'This sort of sultry weather makes me feel incredibly sexy. No wonder in Africa they do nothing but fuck.' He clasped my ankle in a hand, squeezed it and then began gently to stroke it with the ball of his thumb. I pulled my leg away.

'What's the matter? Don't you like me to do that?'

'No.' I could feel my heart stumbling in my chest.

'How about this?' He raised himself and leaned over to put a hand on my thigh. Once more he first squeezed, then stroked.

Horrified, I realised that I was getting an erection. 'Stop it!'

Suddenly he was on top of me. I tried to push him off but could not do so. His mouth descended on mine and, before I had clenched my teeth, for a moment I felt his tongue. His hand went down to my cock.

Then, like a candle in a gale, all my resistance was extinguished.

Well, you enjoyed that, didn't you?' Through the window I could see lightning zigzag down the sky. Almost immediately there was a splutter of thunder. Then I heard the rain, as noisy as hail, on the terrace beneath.

'No. No!' I was seething with mortification and rage.

'Of course you enjoyed it! You did, you did! Otherwise you would never have come!'

'Oh, get off!' I tried to shove him off the bed; but he only laughed, put his arms round me and once more

[127]

hugged me to him. Then, struggling, I managed to strike him a glancing blow on the cheek.

'Careful, careful,' he admonished me, still laughing.

At long last he released me and got off the bed. He tweaked at his boxer shorts, which were sticking to him. 'I'll have to wear these tomorrow with all this spunk on them. Violetta's washing my other pair. Ugh! Perhaps I'd better give them a wash now and hope they'll be dry by the morning.'

I was thinking: Oh, God! I can't let Violetta see these pyjama trousers.

'Well, perhaps now I'll be able to sleep.'

He gave me a little ironic bow and then blew me a kiss, equally ironic, before quitting the room.

I myself could not sleep. For a long time I watched and listened to the storm. Then, when at last it was over, and the only sound was the gentle shush-shushing of the rain, I listened for the return of Ma and Tim. I had a crazy longing to rush up to Ma, a child tormented by guilt for his misdemeanour, and to cry out to her, 'Forgive me, forgive me! I'm sorry, I'm so sorry, I didn't mean to do it.'

Eventually, at almost three o'clock, I heard them come in. Clearly drunk or at least tipsy, they made no effort to be quiet. Ma must have slipped on her way up the stairs, since there was a sudden thud and clatter, followed by Tim saying: 'Whoa! Whoa! Be careful.'

Then Ma was laughing. 'Oh, Tim, Tim, Tim! You really are priceless. Utterly priceless.'

Were they now going to fuck, as Bob had predicted?

I got out of bed and stood at the window, staring out at the lake. The air had become suddenly damp and chill. I shivered and shivered again.

[128]

26

Ma and Tim did not appear for breakfast.

I was the first down, my head throbbing and my stomach unsettled. It might have been I, and not Ma and Tim, who had returned home drunk in the early hours. Maria, setting down a cup of coffee before me, seemed to peer at me with unusual intensity through her short-sighted eyes. At once my guilt persuaded me that, somehow, by some miracle of intuition, she had guessed what had happened between Bob and me the previous evening.

At the door to the kitchen, she turned: Did I want an egg?

I shook my head and muttered: '*Grazie.*'

The rolls, brought up by her from the bakery that same morning, were wonderfully fresh. But for once, as I chewed on the end of one, I felt none of the usual pleasure. The coffee tasted unpleasantly bitter.

It was as I was about to get up from the table that Bob appeared. Cheerfully he greeted me: 'Hello! What a difference that storm has made! It's going to be a wonderful day.'

I said nothing, as he sat down opposite me and drew his napkin out of its ring.

Then, as on the night before, all my resistance suddenly expired, even though I had no intention that it should do so. I looked up at him and eventually gave him a hesitant smile.

'Did you solve the problem of your pyjamas?' he

asked. When I did not reply, he went on: 'My pants seem to be okay. I washed them in cold water and then left them to dry on the towel rail. So Violetta will be spared any shock.'

'What do you want to do today?'

'Oh, I think I'd like another go at swimming. It's absurd that I can't pick up the knack.'

'In the hotel pool?'

'Why not?'

'We might meet Tim's friend.'

'So what?'

Aaron Platz was not by the pool. The only people using it were three German girls in their early teens, with large bosoms and bottoms and beautifully bronzed skins. While I lay out in a deck-chair after my swim, reading *Apollo*, Bob tried to get off with them. But he was hardly successful. They laughed derisively when he cautiously waded in at the shallow end, and they laughed even more when, one foot on the bottom, he attempted a clumsy breast-stroke. Eventually, hauling himself out, he went and lay near the chairs on which they were sitting. '*Guten Morgen*,' he said.

'Good morning, good afternoon, good evening, good night,' one of the girls responded. Then all of them went off into shrieks of laughter.

'So you speak English?'

Another of the girls replied: '*Et aussi je parle français.*'

After some more of this, Bob gave up. Dragging his towel disconsolately behind him, he trailed over to me. 'Cheeky little bitches! They have far too high an opinion of themselves. Only one of them is in the least bit BW.'

'BW?'

'Bedworthy. Haven't you heard that before?'

[130]

'Nope.'

'Oh, God, you're innocent!'

ide by side we sauntered back along the rim of the
ke. People, many of them German, French or English,
natted at the tables set out between the cafés and the
ater. Others wandered past us. Then, all at once,
oming towards us with an oddly stumbling gait, I saw
he middle-aged American whom I now knew to be
alled Aaron Platz. He gave a little start when he
ecognised us, slowed his pace, and attempted a ner-
ous smile. 'Good afternoon,' he said, although Tim
ad never introduced us to him.

Saying nothing, we walked past, our heads averted.

Then, to my embarrassment, Bob burst into a high-
itched cackle of laughter. He turned. 'Oh, my dear!'
e called out after the American, in a whooping falsetto.

Head lowered, Aaron Platz hurried on.

Vhen we returned to the villa, Ma and Tim were out
n the terrace, glasses before them and the cocktail
naker between them. Ma was in her skimpy bathing
ostume, Tim in only shorts. They looked exhausted,
ney looked happy. Bob must have been right. After
heir row, they must have had an orgy of fucking.

Ma stretched luxuriously. 'Beautiful day, beautiful
ay!' she trilled out. Then she asked: 'What time is it?'

Bob looked at his cheap watch, its leather strap
ayed. 'Almost quarter to one.'

'Oh, good! I'm tremendously hungry. I suppose it's
ecause I missed any breakfast. I'd better go up and
ut on some clothes. I don't want to shock old Maria.'
.s she passed Bob on her way to the door into the

sitting-room, she stared appraisingly at him. Then sh
said: 'Your skin's bright red. You look like a lobster.'

'Would you like to eat me?'

'God forbid! I can't think of anything I'd like to e
less.'

Bob glanced over to me and winked.

'So what have you two been up to?' Tim aske
running a hand lovingly over a sunburned should
and then across his chest. 'By the time we got dow
you had vanished.'

I told him about our trip to the pool of the Hot
Serbelloni. I wondered if he would ask if we had see
Aaron Platz, but he did not do so.

'Would you like one of these martinis?' he asked.

'Why not?'

'In that case, perhaps Bob could fetch you a glas
And for himself too, if he wants to join us.'

Bob lumbered to his feet with a sigh and went in
the sitting-room.

'Do you ever realise how lucky you are?' Tim asked

'Lucky?'

'You've been to so many places and yet you're only
what? – seventeen.'

'Yes, I suppose I am lucky in that.'

In an acrid, accusatory tone he went on: 'I'd nev
been abroad until I was twenty-three.' Clearly he ha
forgotten that he had only recently told us that h
parents had moved to Alassio with him when he was
child. Bob and I had already caught him out in
number of such lies. 'And then it was to Dieppe. Th
is only my third visit abroad, you know. I was luc
that a, er, friend gave me a few months in Floren
some time back . . . But, that apart, if it hadn't been f
your mother . . . It's not easy to be beholden.'

I didn't know what to say. 'It's not necessary to fe

eholden,' I eventually got out. 'Why should you? Ma kes your company, and if you can't afford to pay, then he's . . .' I broke off.

'I can understand how people can become commu- ists. Life is so unjust. But of course, even in a com- munist state, the injustices continue. In the Soviet 'nion, Bob would be privileged because he's so clever. nd your mother would be privileged because she's so eautiful – some commissar or other would see to that.'

'And you would be privileged because you're so ood-looking – some female commissar or other would ee to that too. I'm the only one of us who would not e privileged.'

He did not laugh. With a sombre, brooding xpression, he stared down towards the glittering lake elow us.

'I try not to be resentful. But you and even Bob have ad it so easy. Prep school, public school, university to llow. Good job after that. You're still a schoolboy and et you were able to buy that blue silk sweater.'

Bob appeared, a glass in either hand. 'Are these the ght ones?' he asked.

'No, not really,' Tim said. 'Those are for champagne. ut it doesn't really matter.' He took the glasses from ob, placed them on the table, and then began to pour ut two martinis from the art deco cocktail shaker. Still ouring, he said: 'I've just been telling your chum here hat lucky buggers both of you are.'

'Are we?' Bob said, extending a hand to take the glass ffered to him.

'I was born in Brixton,' Tim said. 'I left school – the cal grammar school – when I was sixteen. I was already ying to better myself, and so all the boys – bless their vious little hearts – made fun of me because of what ey called my "posh" accent. My first job was as a sales

[133]

assistant at Barker's. I may even – who knows? – hav
served that aunt of yours. Groceries, that was m
department – the cheese counter. I used to travel t
Kensington and back by bus and Inner Circle. I couldn
afford even a room of my own. I lived with the family.'

'Why are you telling us all this?' Bob asked.

'Why? Oh, I've no idea. Perhaps because I want t
make you both feel guilty.'

'Well, I don't think you'll succeed,' Bob said.

'No. I daresay not.'

For a while all three of us sat in silence. Then Ma, i
a flowered cotton dress but still barefoot and nc
wearing stockings, appeared in the doorway. 'Lunch
ready,' she said. She looked at us in turn. Then sh
exclaimed: 'How glum you all look!'

27

This morning, Noreen was gardening. She was nc
gardening strenuously but, looking out of the bac
window of the shop, I was amazed that she should b
gardening at all. For a while, secateurs in knobbl
hand, she dead-headed the roses. Then, kneeling o
the mat which she always brings out for this task, sh
set about weeding the herbaceous border which sh
herself created three – or was it four? – summers ag
Could a solitary gold injection have had so rapid an
so potent an effect? Or was this a case of what D
Lewes calls 'the placebo factor' working a miracle? Sh
has always been suggestible.

Eventually I threw open the window and called out to her: 'Don't overdo it! Don't tire yourself!'

'Oh, I feel marvellous. Terrific.'

Someone had entered the shop. I closed the window and turned to deal with him. He was a young man in jeans, a sweat-shirt and Doc Martens, with a coloured cloth bound, pirate-wise, round his head, who asked if I stocked any military insignia. I told him that I didn't. He walked out of the shop without another word.

When I have closed up the shop and go through the door which leads from it to the sitting-room, in order to join Noreen for luncheon, I am surprised that the table is unlaid and that there is no sign of her. She is usually so punctilious.

'Noreen!' I call. 'Darling! Where are you?'

'Upstairs!' Her voice is oddly muffled.

'Are you all right?' I begin to climb the narrow, steep stairs. When we bought this Elizabethan cottage, we never thought that one day Noreen would be an invalid.

'Noreen!'

She is lying on the double bed, which we no longer share, since she has become so restless a sleeper. She is on her back, staring up at the ceiling.

'I think I rather overdid things,' she tells me, turning her head to give me a weak, apologetic smile. 'I felt wonderful. Now I feel awful.' She struggles to get off the bed. 'I'll get the lunch.'

'You'll do no such thing. You just rest here and I'll get it. I can bring a tray up.'

'No, darling . . .' Her protest is feeble. She looks extraordinarily, worryingly pale.

It is not much trouble to prepare the luncheon. We never eat anything other than a bowl of soup each,

some salad and some French bread and cheese. There
is always wine but we drink sparingly. I carry up the
tray and place it on the bedside table. Then I draw up a
chair for myself.

Suddenly, I do not know why, I am certain that what
has made this change in Noreen has not been only the
gardening, perhaps has not been the gardening at all. I
gaze at her and briefly she gazes back at me, her glass
of Muscadet almost touching her lips. Then she says:
'Darling, I have a confession to make.'

'Yes?'

'Don't be cross. Promise not to be cross.'

'Of course I won't be cross.'

'I looked in your desk. I found it. Read it. I mean,
read what concerned you and me.'

I am astounded. It is, as far as I know, the first time
that she has ever violated my privacy in such a way. I
have never violated hers. 'But Noreen, how – how
could you?'

'Yes, I know. It was terrible of me. But I knew that
something was on your mind, something was worrying
you. There was that time – do you remember? – when I
came into the room and you threw something, in such
a guilty way, into the drawer of your desk and then
pushed it shut . . . That, well, alerted me.' She gulps
from the glass. 'So I came to feel that I – I had to know,
just had to know.' She looks over to me, her eyes
apprehensive and wary. 'Do you forgive me?'

'Of course I do. Of course! But, oh, I do wish . . . I
didn't want you to know what was happening. I
wanted to keep it from you.'

'He's going to destroy us,' she says. 'That's what he
always wanted to do and now, after all these years . . .'
She has never liked Bob. Just as he has always been
jealous of her, so perhaps she has been jealous of him.

[136]

'I have to appeal to him,' I say. 'I must go and see him. That's what I'm planning.'

'He won't listen to any appeals,' she says bitterly.

'I don't see why not.' But, with a feeling of despair, I wonder if she may not be right. 'After all, those chapters could easily be removed from his book. The book won't suffer all that much . . . It's rather a good book,' I add.

'Well, he's always been clever – so that's not surprising.'

'I don't want you to worry about it. Worry is the worst thing for you.'

She laughs. 'I can hardly not worry. I just can't go through the whole business again. And you can't. Even more, you can't.'

I shrug. 'Let's see how he responds.'

Now it is past eleven o'clock and she has long since gone up to bed. I sit down here, the typescript on my knees. I wonder if there is any chance of getting him to do what Noreen and I want. I think of all the consequences if the press discovers where I am and what has happened to me and if, once again, we have to move on and remake ourselves.

Our two desks are side by side, hers and mine. As I replace the typescript in my desk, I turn, on an impulse, to hers and lift its lid. There, among a jumble of papers, is the glitterwax rose, as it used once to lie among a jumble of papers, tubes of paint, brushes and pens and pencils in her desk in the Black Box.

I pick up the glitterwax rose and weigh it in my palm. Then I raise it to my nostrils and again breathe in that faint smell of paraffin after all these years. It is the smell – yes, I am convinced of it – which establishes the link for me. The glitterwax rose is in my hand; and there, in my memory, are the scorched roses lying on the top of the incinerator. The glitterwax rose is the symbol of the love which has somehow survived all these long, often troubled years which Noreen and I have spent together. The burnt roses are the symbol of Bob's lovelessness in Ma's rejection of him.

I place the glitterwax rose back where it was. With strange persistence, that faint smell of paraffin still lingers on my hand and even in my nostrils.

28

I think that I can remember the day when, like a spore of dry rot or like the virus of some deadly disease, the idea of It first entered not so much my mind or my heart but my bloodstream.

The four of us had driven into Milan, the constant swerving round the hairpin bends at the southern end of the lake making Bob's face go yellow and sweaty with car-sickness. 'Do you think you could drive a little slower, Tim?' I eventually suggested. 'Bob's not feeling all that well.'

Ma snapped: 'The faster we go, the sooner it'll be over for him. In any case,' she added, 'I don't want to be late for my hair appointment.' She looked at her watch. 'Oh, God! We're only just going to make it.'

When we had parked the car by the hairdresser's, Ma turned to Bob and me. 'You two had better go off on your own. You'll be far happier like that and we'll also

[138]

be far happier. Let's meet here at about five thirty. All right?'

'That's fine,' I said.

When Tim and Ma had disappeared into the hairdresser's, Bob said: 'The first thing I must do is revive myself with a drink. Let's go into that café over there.'

He ordered a brandy, in the Italian which, to my shame, he was already beginning to acquire with such ease, and I a coffee. Having gulped at the brandy, he said: 'What a bitch!'

There was no reason to ask to whom he was referring. For the first time, when he spoke disparagingly of Ma, I felt no impulse to argue with him, much less to show any indignation or anger.

'Do you think The One and Only's going to sit in the hairdresser's while her hair's being done?'

'Quite possibly,' I answered. 'That way she can be sure he doesn't get into any mischief.'

'Does he ever pay for anything for himself, let alone for her?'

'Can't afford to. He's broke. I told you how Dad used to call him a scrounger. And a gigolo. And a lounge lizard.' I could hear the contemptuous tone with which Dad would say all three of these things.

'She must be spending a fortune on him. Is she that rich?'

'I don't really know how rich she is. She's always complaining that Aunt Bertha left her only the house, not any money. But I don't believe that. She's terribly extravagant. The villa is costing her a fortune.'

'It was typical that she and he had a first-class sleeper, while you and I had to sit up hard class. I'm amazed you didn't complain.'

I didn't give him the true answer: I've got used to not

complaining. Instead I merely shrugged, drained my coffee and said: 'Let's go.'

As we wandered through the streets of Milan, peering into shop windows, I suddenly, against my will, began to think of the night of the storm and of his body heaving and thrusting close to mine. I could even feel the oppressive heat, and smell the rain. The unbidden memory made me feel slightly nauseated; and yet, at the same time, I longed to be away from Milan, back in the villa, once more on the bed, with our arms around each other.

'You're very silent.'

'Am I?'

'A lira for your thoughts.'

'Oh, they're not worth that. My mind was really blank.'

He lowered his head, then turned it, to look up at me. There was a mischievous, provocative expression on his face. Could he have guessed those thoughts?

Eventually we wandered into the cathedral and climbed, breathing more and more strenuously, up on to its roof. Suddenly, forsaking the walkway, Bob clambered over a low wall, scampered, almost on all fours, up a steep, slithery incline and then embraced a small, elaborately decorated finial. All the other tourists halted and gazed at him in apprehension. Then a custodian appeared and, frantically waving his arms, began to shout in a yelping falsetto. When Bob had returned to the walkway, the custodian told us to descend at once – *immediatamente, subito!* He had a small, pointed, reddish beard, which wagged in fury. As we started down the spiral staircase, he shouted after us: *'Cretini! Scemi!'* Why the plural? I had done nothing amiss.

*

When we eventually met up with them, Ma and Tim were loaded with shopping. 'Everything's wildly expensive,' Ma said. 'But the Italians have such wonderful taste – even better than the French. There were so many things I just couldn't resist. And I felt that it wasn't fair to buy things only for myself, and so Tim got the benefit. Lucky boy! Oh, and I got something for you too,' she added, diving into one of her many shopping bags and handing me a small packet. When I opened it, I found that it contained six handkerchiefs. 'Linen,' she said. 'With an M on each. You seem to lose all your handkerchiefs, I can't imagine how.'

I mumbled my thanks.

'And here's a little something for you.'

Bob's present was a pair of boxer shorts. She must have noticed that he had brought only those two pairs with him.

'What did Mrs Frost buy you?' Bob asked Tim, when the car, having repeatedly refused to respond to the self-starter, eventually lurched off.

'What did she buy me?' Tim put up a hand and adjusted the mirror. I could now see the smirk on his handsome, vacant face. 'Well, first and foremost, there's this watch.' He held up his wrist. 'It's actually French, not Italian. Longines. Isn't it elegant?'

'I suppose it's gold,' Bob said, nudging my knee with his.

'Well, as a matter of fact, yes it is. Then she bought me a cigarette case because she complains that, whenever I offer her a fag, it's from a crushed packet.'

'Also gold?' Bob asked.

'Yes. Yes, that's right.'

'What else?' Bob prompted.

'Oh, some shirts. And – let me see – a sports jacket. And a polo-neck sweater. Like Mervyn's,' he added with satisfaction. 'Silk. But a wonderful shade of burgundy and not that insipid blue . . . So I won't have to borrow his any more. Does that relieve you, Mervyn?' He laughed.

I, too, managed to laugh. 'Yes, it does.'

After our return, I had a shower. Then, since there was at least an hour before dinner would be served, I lay out on my bed, in only my underpants, and listened to a performance of Respighi's 'The Pines of Rome' on the wireless which stood on a table by the window.

The door opened. For minutes now I had been willing and yet dreading its opening.

'What are you doing?'

'Nothing. Listening to some music. Respighi.'

'Never heard of him.'

'He's very popular in Italy.' Suddenly it had become an effort to breathe.

'Don't you want to go down for a drink?'

'Not very much. I feel angry with them.'

'With both of them?'

'Well, more with Ma. What a fool she's making of herself. One can't really blame The One and Only. If she wants to give him all those things, it's natural he should take them from her.'

He laughed. Then he sat down on the end of my bed. 'Perhaps one day I'll be able to find some older woman to keep me in the state to which I'm not accustomed.'

'I doubt it. Let's face it, you're not really the type.'

He clambered on to the bed and then, on all fours, crept up it towards me. He might have been a huge cat. He clasped both my wrists, one in each hand, and then

[142]

lowered his mouth to mine. 'This time I'm really going to kiss you.'

I shook my head from side to side. 'No. No!' Somehow kissing me seemed a greater violation than anything else that he might do to me.

He pressed his mouth on to mine. I thought I would gag. Then he raised his head, looked down at me, laughed. 'Why do you pretend you don't like this?'

'I'm not pretending.'

'Of course you are.'

Still gripping my right wrist, he released the left in order to tug my underpants downwards.

'Oh, stop it! Stop! Ma might come in.'

'Let her! Do her good.'

So, once again, it happened.

After it was over, I sat moodily on the window sill, in my underpants and nothing else, while he lay out on the bed. His hair was tousled, his face flushed. There was a red crease down the left side of his chest.

'I wonder how much money she spent.'

I shrugged.

'She must have spent a fortune. A gold watch *and* a gold cigarette case. And what did we get? Some handkerchiefs for you, some underpants for me. What romantic presents! What generous presents!'

I brooded on it. Then I muttered: 'It makes me sick.'

'I'm not surprised. If she goes on this way, there'll be nothing left for you.'

'Nothing of what?'

'Of cash, idiot! Have you any money of your own?'

'What do you mean?'

'Well, did that aunt, or great-aunt, or whatever she

[143]

was, leave you anything? Has anyone left you anything?'

'No. Of course not.' It was the first time that I had given it any thought.

'Why of course not? Yours seems to be a family in which a lot of money keeps circulating.'

'You've got it wrong,' I said wearily. 'Mine is a family in which people spend money. That's not the same as having it.'

'Your mother stinks of money.' He swung his legs off the bed. 'But how long do you think she can go on in this way?'

'What do you mean?'

'"What do you mean?"' Cruelly he mimicked me. 'What I mean is that, by the time you really need some money, there'll just be none left. So far from your mother being able to help you out, you'll be slaving in some putrid job to help her out.'

Gloomily, I stared down at the lake. A faint mist was rising, as it often did at that hour of dusk, and with it, as always, came a smell of decay, why I never knew.

'You have the perfect motive, you know.'

'The perfect motive? For what?' But I think that I already knew the answer.

'For bumping her off.' Then he laughed as though to say: This is all a joke.

'You're crazy!'

'Not at all. Why should you let her fritter away a lot of money which she never earned? Soon she'll probably have to mortgage that house. Eventually she'll probably have to sell it. And then where will you be? In the *ministra* – as they say in these parts of the world.'

'Oh, shut up!'

He jumped off the bed and came over to the window.

[144]

He lowered himself on to the sill beside me and also looked down at the lake. 'We must think how best to do it,' he said. Again he gave that laugh, intended to say: This is all a joke, of course. 'With all that water, it's a pity one can't just drown her in it. But that might present too many problems. We must think of something better.'

'I'm going to get dressed. And have a shower.' I had already had a shower before we had made love; but now I felt dirty. I could not face Ma feeling like that.

'Shall I join you in the shower?'

'Certainly not!' At the door to the bathroom I turned: 'Beat it!'

'Okay! . . . See you below.'

Under the shower, the water only lukewarm because Ma must have used up most of what was in the hot tank, I began for the first time to think, with a mingling of terror, excitement and guilt, of the possibility of It. The best way that I can describe this tumultuous mingling of emotions is to say that it was as though a black, savage bird, long sleeping, had all at once aroused itself within me, unsheathed its talons and begun to flap its wings.

Strangely, it was with exactly the same tumultuous mingling of terror, excitement and guilt that I had now come to think of Bob and myself making our greedy, clumsy love.

29

The antiquated Citroën was adamant in refusing to respond to the self-starter; and even when Tim used the handle, it was a long time before it wheezed and spluttered into life. Tim looked at his hands. They were streaked with grease. 'Oh, God, look at my hands. I'll never get this off. What will the Traceys think of me, my hands filthy?'

'You can explain,' Ma said.

Tim rushed off to wash his hands, while we sat in the car, waiting for him.

'I'll have to speak to them,' Ma said. 'They' or 'them' always meant the owners of the villa. She was going to speak to them not merely about the car but also about such things as the wireless in the sitting-room, which had an exasperating habit of constantly fading; about the vacuum-cleaner, which from time to time vomited out dust instead of sucking it in; and about the hot-water system, which did not allow her constantly to run hot water while she soaked in the bath for as much as an hour on end.

'That's a bit better,' Tim said, returning. 'I ought really to have changed my shirt. It's got a smudge on one cuff. Of course, it had to be one of the new silk ones.'

'Oh, no!' Ma cried out. 'Not one of those!'

'Yes, I'm afraid so.' He laughed. 'You'll just have to buy me another.'

'I'll do nothing of the kind. I've run through almost all my traveller's cheques.'

'Well, wire your bank to transfer some cash.' The car began to move off.

'I'm not sure there's all that much to transfer.'

'It's always people with money who constantly complain they have none.'

'Remind me to show you my pass-book.'

'This car is a disgrace,' Tim said, changing the gears with a terrible scrunching. 'It's due for the scrap-heap.'

'Yes, I'm going to speak to them about it. When they said they were leaving us a Citroën, I thought of one of those black police cars you see in French films. I never thought for one moment that it would be a beat-up wreck like this.'

Ma had had an introduction to the people who had invited us over for drinks. An elderly couple, white-haired, tall and stiff, they had spent the last ten years or so on landscaping the hillside behind their villa, to spectacular effect. 'It's old money,' Ma had said of them. In her eyes, old money was always superior to new. 'He's never done a day's work in his whole life, I gather.'

There was an immediate awkwardness when Mrs Tracey, having greeted Ma, then turned to Tim beside her and exclaimed: 'And this must be your son!' But Ma passed it off with a tinkle of laughter: 'Oh, dear me, no! Do I really look old enough to be his mother? No, he's just a friend, a very dear friend. Timothy – Timothy Packer. This one here – this is my son. Mervyn. And that one there is Mervyn's friend, Bob. It's just as well to get these things straight, isn't it?'

Mrs Tracey gave a taut, wintry smile. Then she began

[147]

to introduce us to her other guests. Some were English, staying at the more expensive of the hotels round the lake, others were Italian, owners of summer villas.

'Do you speak Italian?' Mr Tracey asked Ma.

'A little!' By now, Ma had given up the pretence that she was adept at the language.

'In any case, *non monta!* Most of the Italians here speak English. Usually learned from their English nannies.'

Ma looked around her. 'This garden is heaven, absolute heaven. I gather you put in years of work to get it as it is.'

'Yes,' Mr Tracey confirmed with satisfaction. 'And we started absolutely from scratch.'

'A miracle,' Ma said. 'If you come over to our rented villa – as I hope you will soon – you will see how *not* to plan a garden. There are no vistas, none at all. Everything so crowded. Everything so garish. Vulgar, I'm afraid.'

Mr Tracey frowned and put a long, bony finger to his lips. 'Sh! The lady over there – the one with the Pekinese – is the niece of your landlady.'

'Oh, dear!' Ma's laughter pealed out.

It was easy to see that Mr Tracey, for all his air of formidable coldness, was taken with her. He began to ask her if she had visited this or that church or museum. Ma had little interest in either art or architecture, but she now kept answering: 'Alas, I've still not been there,' or 'That's one of the things I most want to see,' or 'We set out for it but then our wretched car went and had a puncture.' Soon, Mr Tracey was offering to take her on a sightseeing tour in his own car – 'It's an Alfa Romeo – almost brand new. The last word in comfort.'

Tim, leaning over the balustrade of the terrace, was talking vivaciously to a beautiful young girl who, from

[148]

he back, might have been mistaken for a beautiful
young boy, so slim was her figure and so short was her
hair. I wondered if Ma would notice them and try to
get Tim away. But she was too much taken up with Mr
Tracey.

Bob came over to me, where I stood sheepishly alone.
He had been talking to an elderly man in a white linen
suit and panama hat, who kept sneezing into a handkerchief; but the man, having grown fidgety – I could
hear Bob going on about the geology of the district –
eventually excused himself by saying that he would
have to go indoors, since he was suffering so much
from his hay-fever.

'Shall I come with you?' Bob asked.

'Oh, no, no!' the old man replied quickly, in panic. 'I
wouldn't dream of dragging you indoors on a day as
beautiful as this.'

Bob and I then wandered away from the others, up
the hillside and into a copse. A Siamese cat emerged
from the undergrowth and coquettishly sidled up to us.
Bob stooped and stroked it under the chin. It stood on
tiptoe, the bell on its velveteen collar tinkling, and
arched its neck for him. 'You're beautiful,' he told it.
'Far more beautiful than anyone down there.' Then he
said to me: 'Dreadful people. When I see people like
that, I think, "Better dead," like that doctor in *The
Doctor's Dilemma*. Better dead. One could say that of so
many people. Which reminds me. I suddenly thought
in the car of another way of doing it. One could do
something to the brakes. Tim and your mother both go
on and on about how ancient that car is, how unrelia-
ble. No one would think anything of it if the brakes
failed.' He gave an impish grin. 'I'm sure I could
arrange it. I'm good at that sort of thing. You know
that.'

'We'd better go back. They'll be wondering what ha
happened to us.'

I was desperate to ignore what, in seeming jest, h
had proposed. Yet later, against my will, my mind kep
slithering back to it, just as it kept slithering back to th
thought of Bob's body intertwined with my own.

30

Jack stands over me, while I weed the herbaceous
border.

Noreen once said that he looked as if he had got
squashed in a door. His shoulders, hips and head are
all extremely narrow, and they seem even narrower
because he is almost six-and-a-half foot tall. His high
forehead has three deep furrows in it, and furrows no
less deep run from either side of his pointed nose to
either side of his thin-lipped mouth.

'I wish you'd give me your advice,' he says, pleading
with me now. 'I trust you. I feel that you have so much
– so much *judgement*, where moral problems are
concerned.'

'I really don't know what to say.' Nor do I.

Now he squats beside me, all jutting chin and jutting
knees and elbows. He twists his wide wedding-ring
round its finger. 'In a way, I still love Moira. I really do
But it's years since I was in love with her. She's been a
good wife to me and I like to think that, until now, I've
been a good husband to her. But the sex thing ended
ages ago between us – her decision – and she now lives

a life strangely detached from mine. Well, you may have noticed that yourself.'

I rub some soil off my fingers. I look sideways at him, and the obliquity of my gaze seems merely part of the obliquity of my whole stance in regard to his problem. I like him and I want to help him. But I feel that I am as incompetent to give him advice about whether he should precipitate a scandal or not as I should be incompetent to give him advice as to how to invest his money.

'Don't do anything irrevocable without a lot of thought,' I eventually get out.

Now he is impatient with me, even exasperated. 'Do you think I haven't already given this a lot of thought? I lie awake night after night – thank goodness Moira and I no longer share a room – or I get up in the early hours and brood over a cup of tea in the kitchen. It's terrible to know that, whatever conclusion one reaches, one has got to hurt someone. The point is: who will I hurt the most? Moira has her own life – all that voluntary work of hers and her amateur dramatics. To be without me might hurt her *amour propre* but it wouldn't hurt her essential self. Whereas . . . I don't see how Iris would really get through without me. She's had a wretched life, you know.'

'Yes, I know.'

Round and round we go.

'What does Noreen think?'

'I've not really discussed it with her.' But that is untrue. She thinks that Jack should stick with his wife. Most wives think that of most errant husbands.

'I wish you would discuss it with her.'

'I will. When she's better. She's in so much pain at present. The first gold injection seemed to have a miraculous effect, but since then . . .'

'It's tough on her,' he says. But he is not really thinking about Noreen. He is thinking only about the toughness of the decision ahead of him.

Eventually I walk with him up the lawn and out to the front of the house, where he has left his bicycle.

'Don't you have a lock?'

He gives a weak smile as he gets astride it. 'I try to make it my policy to trust people,' he says.

I wonder if Moira makes it her policy to trust him.

'When Noreen is better, we must have a rubber of bridge.'

'That would be lovely,' I reply. I hate playing bridge with Moira and Jack. They make one realise the full, dire meaning of the phrase 'vicarage bridge'.

When he has swayed off on the rusty, old-fashioned bicycle with the high saddle and handle-bars, I go up to see how Noreen is. She is lying with her face to the wall, her knees drawn up. Perhaps she is asleep? But she turns over at the sound of my entrance.

'What did he want?'

'My advice. Which I can longer give him. I just don't feel competent any longer.'

'Things haven't changed. And you haven't changed. What's the difference?'

'I'd feel such a hypocrite.'

'We're all hypocrites to some degree or another. Jack certainly is.'

It is unlike her to be so cynical.

'Can I get you anything?'

As though she has not heard me, she says: 'I keep thinking about that book of his. And I keep asking myself: Why, why, why? Why, after so many years, should he do this to us?'

'He seems to hate us,' I say.

[152]

31

Tim and Ma had another squabble, so public, out on the terrace, and so noisy that yet again I was sickened by the gaudy thread of exhibitionism which flashed through almost all their behaviour together. Just as they would fondle and even kiss each other not merely in the house and on the terrace but also in restaurants and cafés or walking by the lake, so too they would savage each other with an equal craving to be heard and seen.

Bob and I were once again upstairs in my room, this time playing not chess but bezique ('You've just got to face it,' Bob had said, 'you're not up to chess') when we heard the voices. 'Oh, lord,' Bob said, 'not again! What will those two biddies next door think?'

'They'll think what they must have been thinking for a long time.'

Loud and clear, I could hear Tim's: 'You stupid cunt!', followed by Ma's: 'How dare you speak to me like that! How dare you!'

I put my hands over my ears. 'What I can't bear is the mess,' I said. 'Wherever Ma goes and whatever she does, there has to be mess. Day after day Maria and Violetta tidy up, and day after day she turns everything into a mess again.' I was thinking of the bathing towel which, returning from the hotel swimming pool, she would abandon over a chair in the hall; of the shoes which she would kick off on the terrace and then forget; of the cigarette-ash scattered over the parquet and the cigarettes stubbed out in teacups or saucers. I was also

[153]

thinking of the emotional mess in which she lived, passion and hate and jealousy slopping out in all directions.

'*Delenda est,*' Bob said, fanning his cards. His tone was matter-of-fact. He might have been talking of the putting down of a cat or a dog. 'But how? There's the car idea. Or there's poison. How about some poisoned chocolates? She's always guzzling chocolates.' He began to tell me of a recent murder case, in which a poisoned chocolate had been the means chosen by a retired army officer to murder his neighbour. But how was the murderer to ensure that his victim ate that particular chocolate and no other? The murderer had held it out: 'Excuse fingers,' he had said. 'With your mother you wouldn't have that problem. Given a box of chocolates, she could be relied on to demolish the lot.' He picked up his cards again. He played one. 'Oxalic acid,' he said. 'That would be a possibility. That's what's used in that novel I've been reading – *Death of My Aunt.* The best thing, of course, would be to give her an injection of insulin. That would leave no traces. But how would we get hold of it?'

Was he joking? Was he being serious? I could not be sure.

Certainly he must have been joking when he went on to speak about the possibility of pushing Ma into the huge oven in the antiquated kitchen and roasting her – 'It would be like the witch in *Hansel and Gretel* – but think of the pong!'

When we eventually went downstairs for dinner, Tim had vanished and Ma was slumped on the sofa, legs up, with a handkerchief pressed to her mouth and nose.

'What's up?' I asked, although I knew perfectly well.

'Oh, Tim's just been horrid to me, perfectly horrid.'

[154]

She gave a small, choking sob into the handkerchief and then put it down in her lap, before stretching out for her glass of neat gin on the rocks. 'Why does he have to be so horrid to me?' she demanded. 'I do so much for him, I constantly spend money on him.'

'Perhaps it would be better if you did less and spent less.'

'It's easy for you to say that! If I weren't so generous, he'd just walk out on me. That Platz creature telephoned from Rome this afternoon. I couldn't help overhearing. Of course he's trying to lure him away. How am I supposed to compete with a millionaire film producer?'

'People say his career is on the skids,' Bob interjected.

Ma glared at him over her upraised glass. 'Would you mind *not* butting in? We're discussing a purely – a purely *f-f-familiable* matter.'

It was then, as she ludicrously stumbled over the non-existent word, that I realised that that gin was not the first, there had been many before it.

I stooped and began to pick up the sheets of the *Daily Sketch* littered around her.

'I do wish you'd find him,' Ma said in a fretful voice, close to tears.

'Oh, I expect he'll be back for dinner. He's unlikely to miss that.'

'Don't, don't be so utterly heartless!' Ma wailed. 'In his present mood, he could do anything.'

I heard a sound in the hall.

'He's back,' I said.

Ma jumped to her feet. 'Tim! Tim! Is that you? Oh, darling, I was so worried – so upset . . .'

Bob looked over to me.

Then, for the first time, I really thought that I could kill her; and really hoped that Bob, who would do it so

[155]

much more efficiently and resourcefully, would kill her for me.

32

In an art bookshop in Milan I had found a copy of the *Studio*. Although it was two months old, it was one that I had not read. With it, I lay out on a deck-chair in the garden.

Bob appeared, in his usual grubby khaki shorts, aertex shirt and gym shoes.

'How about a walk?'

'Where to?'

'Round the lake. Or up into the hills. Where else?'

'Oh, it's too hot. Besides, I want to read this.' I held up the magazine.

'Boring!'

'Not at all. I find *Nature* boring. We're different, that's all.'

'They've gone off. In the car.' Only much later did I detect something conspiratorial in the way he said it.

'Where to?'

'Oh, to visit those friends. What are they called? The ones with the garden and the Siamese cat.'

'Tracey.'

'Tracey. That's right. The One and Only had a letter from the Platz creature this morning,' he added.

'How do you know?'

'I've just peeped into his room.'

'Oh, you haven't! You really are a most terrible little sneak.'

'And you're a most terrible little prig.' He laughed. 'Don't you want to know what was in it?'

'In what?'

'The letter, idiot.'

'No, not really.'

'It was a love-letter, really. Disgusting! It was full of promises as love-letters so often are. Not just promises of undying devotion but promises to do all kinds of wonderful things for Tim.'

'Ma had better not know about it.'

'No. It would send her berserk.' He laughed. 'But perhaps that's a reason for letting her know about it. The berserker, the better!'

I returned to my reading, while he stood beside me, gazing down towards the lake. 'I used to think that lake beautiful,' he eventually sighed. 'But now it only bores me. I really can't wait to get back to England.'

'Thanks!'

'No, I don't really mean that. That must have sounded ungrateful. It's far more fun being here than in Bexhill, I can tell you.'

When he had gone, I tried to concentrate on what I was reading about Burmese glass. But I could not do so. The original virus or the spore – however one looks at it – was beginning to proliferate.

Perhaps Dr Unwin was right when, years later, he speculated about the possibility of demonic possession. Perhaps, when Bob had possessed me on those two occasions in my bedroom, he had possessed more than my body. We had joked together about killing Ma, and it had all been a game – 'I know – we could push her down the stairs,' 'No, no, much better to push her out of her bedroom window, so that it appeared to be suicide,' 'Or down those steps in the garden,' that kind of thing. But now I was beginning seriously to think of killing her.

That previous night I had dreamed of Dad. I was looking up at his swollen, purple face, then down at his feet, the shoes off, the thick woollen socks rucked about his ankles, as he dangled from his Coldstream tie. Then, all at once he was saying to me, in that flat, monochrome voice, which always indicated that he had entered one of his depressions: 'Please, please, beg your mother to come and see me.'

I could not now stop thinking of him. 'It's a dog's life,' he had often said to me, sometimes with a sigh but more often with a smile. His had been a dog's life, largely because of that bitch.

What right had she to live when he was dead?

I had begun to reread the article on Burmese glass, when all at once I heard a distant sound, like a muffled explosion. I hurried to the railings separating the terrace from the precipitous slope below it, and peered down. Why did that sound have that effect on me? Why did my head seem like a balloon on the point of bursting? Why did I feel such an extraordinary mixture of elation and dread? After all, it could merely have been the sound either of quarrying up in the mountains or of blasting to widen the perilously narrow road round the lake. Both were familiar. Had I guessed that something had happened? Had I had some premonition?

I waited there for minutes on end. Then I heard the sirens wailing in the distance. Two black police cars shot into view, lurched round a corner of the road, and disappeared from sight. An ambulance followed more sedately. After that, an eerie silence.

I returned to my deck-chair, I tried to read. But I could not do so. I wanted to descend the hill, race round the lake, discover what had happened.

[158]

A long time later, I heard a car approaching. Again I went to the railings of the terrace. It was one of the black police cars, screeching round one hairpin bend after another.

I ran out into the drive. Tim stepped out of the police car, staggered, would have fallen but for the hand which a policeman put out to support him. His face was extraordinarily pale. There was some dried blood caked round one of his nostrils.

'Are you all right?' I asked. 'What's happened? Where's Ma?'

The three policemen were all talking simultaneously in loud, ringing voices.

'I'm all right. I had a bash on the nose, but I'm all right.'

'Where's Ma?' I repeated. I must have sounded concerned for her safety; but there was only one answer which I really wanted and expected.

'They've taken her to the hospital in Como. They're going to X-ray her arm. But they think nothing's broken. Only a sprain and bruising.'

I hurtled down into an abyss of disappointment.

'Why aren't you with her?' I wanted to ask; and, as though I had indeed put the question, he said: 'The ambulance men told me it was best if I got back here. They said I was in shock. I passed out by the roadside. Rather embarrassing.'

He began to limp into the house.

'What happened?'

'Brakes failed. Just wouldn't respond. That bloody car! Fortunately we were not on the lake side of the road. But in order to avoid an oncoming bus, I had to drive into the gate of one of the villas. The only trouble was that I drove into not only the gate but into the wall as well. That car's a write-off,' he added. 'It's a miracle we both weren't a write-off too.' He put a hand up to his mouth. 'Oh, God, I'm going to be sick!' At that, he rushed to the lavatory.

Suddenly I realised that Bob was standing behind me. I spun round, we stared at each other. Then he grinned.

'Pity,' he said. 'If they'd been fifty yards further on, they'd have gone wham bang into the rock-face.'

Later, much later, after I had gone over to the hospital to see how Ma was, and after I had brought her home in a taxi and after she had screamed at Tim for 'leaving me to my fate, just leaving me, thinking only of yourself', I said to Bob: 'Tell me the truth, Bob. Did you do anything to that car?'

'What do you think?'

'Did you?'

I now wanted him to say: 'Yes, of course, I tampered with the brakes.' If he said that, I should be in no way shocked. I should only be profoundly grateful to him, I should only love him all the more.

But he merely repeated: 'What do you think?' Then he gave that impudent smile of his. 'Thoughts have power. Dreams have power. Wishes have power.'

33

I woke in the middle of the night, consumed by anger as by a raging fire. Once already he had ruined my life now he was set on ruining it again. What was the source of his malevolence? What had I ever done to harm him? Although, with a high wind rattling the window frame, the night was cool, I felt the sweat breaking out on my forehead, under my armpits, between my buttocks. I threw off the blanket, I groaned aloud. From the next-door room – I always leave both her and my door open, in case she needs me – I heard Noreen call out something. But when I called back: Noreen! Is something the matter?', I got the sleep-logged answer: 'All right. Everything all right.'

Now, as I sit in the shop expecting, as I so often do during this period of recession, a customer who never comes, I ask myself yet again: What are you waiting for? Why don't you go and see him? Or, if you don't go to see him, why don't you write to him? You have his address, you know his village, it would be easy to drive from here to there and back in a single morning or a single afternoon. It would be even easier to pick up a pen.

I am afraid of something, that's it. But of what? Of him? Or of myself?

A young girl, trailing a child, comes in. She looks at me and her pretty, open face freezes into concern – or is it alarm?

'Have I caught you at a bad time?' she asks.

If I were truthful, I should answer: 'Yes, a very bad time. At the moment all times are bad.' But I get up from my chair and advance towards her smiling. 'No, no. I've all the time in the world. What can I do to help you?'

'Well, actually – I don't actually – I don't actually

want to buy anything. I, er, actually, want to sel
something.' She puts a hand into the pocket of he
pinafore dress.

These days they all want to sell something.

34

Our last five or six days in Bellagio were surprisingl
peaceful ones.

Tim lavished all his attention on Ma, either throug
guilt for his behaviour at the accident or through fea
that that behaviour might have turned her against him
Supine on the *chaise-longue* in the sitting-room, sh
would jerk her right arm out of its sling, with a winc
of pain (why could she not use her left arm, I ofte
wondered), preparatory to reaching for a cigarette i
the silver box on the table beside her; and at once h
would leap to his feet, pull out the gold cigarette cas
(Fabergé, he had boasted to me one evening when w
were alone together) and a gold cigarette lighter whic
she had also given to him, and then ask: 'Shall I ligh
one for you, darling?' Stooping, he would place the l
cigarette between her lips and then give her a passin
kiss on her cheek or her forehead.

Before, when she prattled on and on, becoming mor
and more inconsequential and silly as she gulped mor
and more gin, he would pick up the newspaper an
begin ostentatiously to read. 'Are you listening to m
Tim?' she would eventually demand, for him to repl
airily: 'Yes, yes, I'm taking in every word.' Now this n
longer happened. Legs outstretched and hands claspe

in his lap, he would gaze steadfastly at her, nod, put his head on one side and give an amused or under- standing smile, would exclaim: 'Oh, really!', 'How amazing!', 'Oh, that's unbelievable!'

Ma loved all this attention: if the pain of the arm was the price, then it was clearly worth it. 'Oh, Tim, what a faithful friend you are!' she would tell him. 'What would I do without you? The One and Only!' To me she would say: 'Isn't he a darling?' or 'What have I done to deserve so much attention?'

In contrast, Bob was perfunctory on all those occasions when, in Tim's absence, Ma asked him to do something. 'Would you be an angel and fetch my book for me from my room?' she asked him after dinner one evening. He pulled a face, which must have been visible to her, sighed and made for the door. 'Hatter's Castle,' she called out after him. When he returned with the book, he chucked it across to her with a flick of the wrist, so that it landed in her lap. 'How can you bear to read such tripe?' he asked. Ma bridled: 'Tripe? It's not tripe at all. It's a serious novel. It had a very good crit in The Observer.' Bob gave a loud, derisive laugh.

It was soon after that that he said to me: 'Your mother is milking her bad arm for all it's worth, isn't she? For God's sake, it isn't broken. I don't believe for one moment that she really needs that sling.' Then he grinned: 'I'd really like to give her a reason for wearing it. In fact, I'd like to break both her arms.'

On the day before our departure, Ma and Tim paid another visit to Como, this time by hired car. They did not suggest that Bob and I should go too.

After we had seen them off, I said: 'It was mean of Ma not to take us!'

'Who wants to trail round with them? That's a deadly town anyway. Now we're free to do exactly what we want. Come on!' He began to race up the stairs, then halted, since I was not following. 'Come *on!*' Reluctantly I began to walk up the stairs. What could he be planning?

He turned the handle of the door to Ma's room, opened it and beckoned to me.

'No, Bob! No! We mustn't go in there.'

'Oh, don't be such a cretin! Why shouldn't we? Come on.'

Such was the force of his will that, dragging step by step, I at last ventured into the room behind him.

He began to pull out drawers, at one moment brandishing a brassière and at another a pair of black silk knickers, rimmed with lace. He held something aloft. 'Do you know what this is?' he asked.

I peered at the object, shook my head.

'A diaphragm, idiot!'

I was none the wiser.

'Don't you know what a diaphragm is? It's what's called "a contraceptive device".' How did he know that? He chucked the diaphragm back into its drawer and then, from the same drawer, produced a large tube. He studied the label. He whistled. He pushed the tube at me. 'Ever seen a contraceptive jelly? I bet you haven't. Now why on earth should that old bitch be worrying so much about contraception? She must be years past it. Perhaps it's just her way of making Tim think she's younger than she is.'

Systematically he examined all Ma's possessions – her dresses, her innumerable pairs of shoes, her medicines and perfumes – while I looked on, at once excited and appalled. I had never indulged in such a scrutiny;

had never even entered her bedroom unless she was there.

Having gone through some letters written by Tim – 'the ass is barely literate' – Bob collapsed on to Ma's bed. Once, twice, he bounced on it. 'This bed is far more comfortable than my bed upstairs. Or yours. And far bigger. Try it!'

I hesitated.

'Oh, come on! Come on!'

I clambered on to the high bed. My heart was thumping. It was as though a huge drum were being beaten inside me. Then he rolled over towards me, put his arms round me, gripped me ferociously.

For a few seconds I tried to struggle free, kicking him on a shin. Then, with a feeling of extraordinary happiness and desolation, the one an integral part of the other, I gave in yet again.

Afterwards, I was terrified that Ma would realise that we had violated not merely her room but her bed. Frantically I pulled at the sheets, patted the pillows. 'Oh, stop that!' Bob said, watching me from a chair. 'She won't notice a thing. She's the least observant woman I know.'

He was right. Ma noticed nothing.

'So what have you two been doing in our absence?' she asked us.

'Boring each other,' Bob replied.

'Why don't you ever go out? You could sit around chatting and reading just as well in England.'

'We often go out,' Bob said. 'You just never notice.'

Ma and Tim had returned laden with purchases. 'We've been terribly extravagant,' she said. What she meant was 'I'. 'Tim couldn't resist the most beautiful cashmere overcoat, perfect for the autumn in London, and I bought myself two evening dresses in a little shop which Tim, not I, noticed. Show them the shoes, Tim!' she commanded. 'You must see his new shoes.'

Delighted to do so, Tim opened the box. The shoes were of suede.

'My father says that no gentleman ever wears suede shoes,' Bob remarked, having glanced at them.

'What nonsense!' Ma exclaimed indignantly. 'I've never heard such nonsense. Your father must have been born in the Dark Ages.'

'Well, yes, he *was* born an awfully long time ago,' Bob admitted.

Looking back now on those weeks in Bellagio, I see that, like some fever which mysteriously ebbs from the patient and then sweeps back to him in an even more virulent form, my hatred of Ma constantly fluctuated. There were times when I even thought of her with admiration and, yes, tenderness.

One of her 'good' days – that was how I thought of those occasions when it seemed as though the sun had all at once, after many weeks, broken through a lowering sky – occurred after the gardener, who also worked next door, told us that one of the two elderly women neighbours was about to have her seventieth birthday. Ma had so often referred to them derisively as 'the devil's dykes' or 'those two Wells of Loneliness'. Now, however, she decided that she must 'do something for them'. Over the wall, she asked them if they would like to come to tea on the day which she now knew to be

hat of the birthday. At first surprised and reluctant,
hen gratified, they accepted.

An excellent cook, although she could rarely be
bothered to do any cooking, Ma supervised Maria in
the baking of a cake and herself saw to its elaborate
icing. There was a moment of fury when Tim tactlessly
pointed out that '*compleanno*', the Italian word for 'birthday', already inscribed in pink lettering, should have
been spelled with two n's, not one, but Ma was pacified
when he told her that the cake was 'a masterpiece, a
little masterpiece'.

The women, both wearing brown lace dresses reaching almost to their ankles and smelling strongly of eau-
de-Cologne, were amazed that Ma should have learned
of the birthday and delighted that she should have
done something about it. Ma could not have been more
charming and gracious, as she pressed cucumber sandwiches on them – 'No English tea is a real English tea
without cucumber sandwiches' – congratulated them
on their English, and listened attentively as they spoke
of their work for animal welfare in the district.

When the women had gone, I had to tell her: 'You
were wonderful!'

She laughed. 'Aren't I always wonderful?'

How could I truthfully answer that question?

I said nothing.

Another of Ma's 'good' days occurred when, lifting the
heavy aluminium kettle off the range, Violetta slipped
and scalded her knee. At a shriek, not from the girl but
from her mother, Ma raced into the kitchen. 'Oh, you
poor darling!' I heard her cry out. Then she switched to
Italian: '*Ah, poveretta, poveretta!*' She grabbed a dish-
cloth and a bottle of olive oil – by now I had joined her

[167]

– and in no time at all was smearing the oil over the scalded knee. 'Tim!' she called. 'Tim! We must get poor little Violetta down to the hospital as quickly as possible!' Her former jealousy over Tim's interest in the girl seemed to have been forgotten; she was genuinely concerned, I was sure. She put an arm round Violetta and began to support her to the front door.

When she returned – Tim was still sulky at having had to drive the hired car to the hospital – it was first to tell Bob and me that she had dropped 'the poor little thing' off at 'that squalid little hovel of theirs by the abattoir' and then to go into the kitchen to tell Maria to go home too. She would herself prepare the evening meal, she announced.

This she did, in the highest of spirits, warbling *'Funicolì, funicolà'* as she rushed about the task.

'Though I say it myself, I really do think that I'm a better cook – or, at least, a more imaginative cook – than our dear old Maria,' she boasted, with justifiable pride, when we had eventually sat down to the meal.

'You're a marvel,' Tim said.

And, for that day at least, it was true.

There were other such 'good' days; or, if not good days, then good hours or even good moments. But even as I was thinking: Dear old Ma, or She's not really all that bad, she would perform some action so stupid, so selfish or so cruel, that, in a fury, I would tell myself We must do It, we *must*! Soon, soon, *soon*! Why the hell are we waiting?

These abrupt shifts in her behaviour and in my attitude to her paralleled the no less abrupt shifts in the weather. From the terrace one would look down on the lake, serene beneath the bluest of skies. Then, in a few minutes, huge, leaden clouds would crowd up over the horizon, a vicious wind would claw at the surface of the water, and a storm would explode around us, in thunder and torrents of rain.

Such a storm occurred on our last day in Bellagio. We had scarcely stepped off the vaporetto from Cadenabbia than we had to race for shelter under the awning of a hairdresser's, which Ma had disdained ever to patronise, preferring to go to Como, or, on one occasion, to Milan. There were, as always, a number of small sailing boats, rowing boats and motor boats out on the lake. To our horror we all at once saw that one of the sailing boats, as though some invisible giant's hand had plucked at it, had capsized. 'Oh, my God!' Ma screeched, putting her hands to her cheeks. Motor boats careered to the rescue. People rushed out from houses, shops and cafés and, unheeding of the deluge, lined the shore. Bob and I joined them, leaving Ma and Tim still beneath the awning. Soon both of us were soaked.

When, later, we heard that two of the three people, all French teenagers, on the boat had been drowned, the first thought that came to me was: Why couldn't the storm have happened yesterday afternoon? Tim had then persuaded Ma to go out in a sailing boat with him. Like Bob, Ma hated the water and could swim only with an effortful and clumsy breast-stroke.

Suddenly, one last memory of those last days in Bellagio comes back to me.

The night was extraordinarily humid and I had been lying awake, wishing for Bob beside me and wondering whether to venture into his room at so late an hour. The last time that I had taken the initiative in that way, he had been furious, first shouting: 'No, no, *no!*' and then, when I had edged nearer and nearer to his bed and had eventually put out a hand, yelling: 'Oh, fuck off! Fuck – bloody – *off!*'

Undecided, I clambered off my bed and crossed over to the open window. A mist was rising off the lake, so that I could see only the houses immediately beneath me, their outlines becoming increasingly nebulous and at last vanishing as they receded on either side of the hoop of the shore. Then, all at once, I realised that there was someone out there, seated on the low wall which separated the terrace from the garden falling away below it. I could see the glow of a cigarette, I could make out a humped shape.

I peered, eyes screwed up.

It was Ma! What on earth was she doing out in the garden so long after we had all gone to bed?

On an impulse I pulled on my dressing-gown and, barefoot, tiptoed down the stairs, through the sitting-room, still reeking of stale cigarette smoke, and out on to the terrace.

'Ma! What are you doing here?'

She put a finger to her lips. 'Sh!' Then she plucked what was left of her cigarette out of its amber holder and flung it over the terrace into the garden below.

'I couldn't sleep either,' I whispered, perching myself on the wall beside her.

With amazement, I now noticed that her cheeks were glistening with tears.

'What's the matter? Has something upset you?'

She only sighed, turning her head away from me.

'Ma! What is it?'

She bent over to scratch at a bare ankle. No doubt one of the mosquitoes which infested the garden at night had bitten her. Then, still bent over, she said:

[170]

Oh, I don't know. It's all so hopeless really. He says he loves me, he constantly says he loves me. But . . . *ut*,' she repeated. She gave a little laugh. 'Why does there always have to be a but?'

'Perhaps he's not really right for you,' I ventured.

'Of course he isn't right for me. But what am I to do, darling?' She put a hand over mine. 'You're too young to understand an infatuation. That's the problem, you see. Your poor old Ma is well and truly infatuated.' Her hand now gripped mine. 'There's no way out. None that I can see. I'm just – just mad about him. The One and Only.' At that she leapt to her feet. 'Sorry, darling. I shouldn't unload my troubles on to you. It's just that for some reason I all at once began to feel blue. It's no fun for a woman when she begins to get old.'

'You're not *old*, Ma.'

'Oh, yes, I am! I am! To him I am. Ancient. As old as the hills.'

At that, without another word, she slipped away from me, entered the drawing-room, vanished.

I sat on, as the mist, clammy and smelling of decay, crept higher and higher. Suddenly I was pierced with a feeling of sorrow: for her, above all for her, but also for Dad, dead now, and yes, for myself, for myself too, although I could not think why.

35

In the dining-car, Ma was suddenly taken ill. She had been talking vivaciously; then, all at once, she put a hand first to her chest and immediately afterwards to her mouth. She gulped, jumped up from the table and rushed out.

Tim got reluctantly to his feet. 'What's the matter with her?'

Bob went on carefully buttering a roll.

I too now got up from my seat. 'Perhaps I'd better go and see.' I felt, at one and the same moment, a sickening terror and a wild joy. These emotions were accompanied by a strange visual hallucination. Everything on the table – the bottles of Orvieto and San Pellegrino, the glasses, the plates, the vase and the flowers in the vase – seemed to be pulsating, as I stared down at them, in time to the ever-increasing speed of my heartbeats. For a moment I thought that I was about to pass out.

'No, no. I'll go.' Tim took a pace and then turned. 'You might ask the waiter to keep my food hot.' He always hated lukewarm food.

I stared at Bob, willing him to acknowledge responsibility for what had taken place; but for a long time, staring out of the window at the darkening countryside, he would not meet my gaze. Then he turned: 'Soon we'll be going through the tunnel again. I found that tremendously exciting the last time. I think it was the most exciting thing of all on this holiday.'

'I hope Ma's all right.' Once again I gazed intently at him and once again he did not return my gaze. I gave a nervous giggle. I put out a hand. I all but touched his, resting on the table between us.

Still staring out of the window, he shrugged. 'Something she's eaten must have disagreed with her.'

Ma later described that journey as 'hell, sheer hell'. All that night, as we crossed Switzerland and then entered

France, she was horribly ill. Still weighed down by dread and yet fizzing with excitement – how could two such contradictory emotions have existed side by side? – I repeatedly made the journey down the swaying train from the hard class to the first class, where she and Tim were once again sharing a sleeper. Somehow the guard had located a French doctor; but, sleepy and ill-tempered, he was of little use. Wrinkling his nose, no doubt in distaste at the nauseating stench of vomit in the little sleeping-car, he said: 'Maybe she eats something not good. Soon she will be better. She must drink water, water, much water.' Ought we to pay him? But he had gone before I could put the question to Tim, who brushed it aside – 'No need to pay him for some perfectly useless advice.'

Meanwhile, rigid in his seat, his head thrown back and his eyes shut, Bob slept through all my to-ings and fro-ings. By dawn Ma was at last better. Face pale, lipstick smudged and sweat beading her forehead, she lay out sleeping on the bunk. Her breathing was effortful.

'She seems to be recovering,' Tim said with a sigh. 'At last. I'm utterly whacked!'

Once again I plunged into an abyss of disappointment. 'What do you think upset her? We were all eating the same things.' Nothing that I said must alert him to the possibility that Bob had been responsible.

He shrugged. 'Who can say? A fly settles on one piece of meat and not on another. That's often how it happens.'

When I returned to our carriage, feeling sweaty and disorientated and reeling with fatigue, Bob was awake. He smiled at me, rubbing the stubble on his chin; then he yawned. 'So? How is she? Still alive?'

'She seems to be better. But it was a really ghastly

night.' I shrugged, pulled a face, stared intently at him
He did not respond. For a while we sat silent, facing
each other, with people still asleep on either side of us
Then I said: 'Come out into the corridor for a moment.'

'Why? What the hell?'

'Come out.' I felt my heartbeats fluttering in my
fingertips.

He followed me out of the carriage. Once again he
yawned, not bothering to raise a hand to his mouth
He edged over to the window and squinted out at the
landscape now beginning to define itself in the first
opaque, grey light of dawn.

'Bob, you must tell me. Did you have anything to do
with Ma's illness?' Now my heartbeats were also ham-
mering in my temples.

'I? I? Did you?'

'Tell me, Bob. If you did . . .' I smiled at him in
complicity and love. 'Well, if you did . . .'

He laughed, throwing back his head. Then he
repeated what he had said to me on that previous
occasion: 'Thoughts have power. Dreams have power.
Wishes have power.'

With that he turned away from me and re-entered
the carriage.

36

There was still a week to go before our return to school.
It seemed only reasonable and only kind that for that
period we should ask Bob to stay with us in the
Campden Hill Square house; but Ma would have none

[174]

of it. 'No, I'm sorry,' she had said in Bellagio, when I had raised the subject with her. 'I've had enough of him. He's so grubby and so gauche. Terribly unappealing. If he were a little more *sortable*, I might feel differently.'

'But, Ma, he's got nowhere to go!'

'What about that holiday home in Worthing or Hastings or wherever it is?'

'He hates it there.'

'Too bad. I can't be blamed for that. It's his parents' responsibility, not mine.' She stared into my face. 'It's no use scowling like that. You've no idea what he's cost me. I really do think that those parents of his could have at least paid his fare. And the amount he ate! Even worse than you.'

'Tim ate quite as much as we did.'

Ma ignored that. 'I'll have to put through a long-distance call to those holiday-home people. Ask him if he has the number or at least an address. If they can't take him, I'll have to get on to the school. He'll just have to arrive there a week early.'

Now Bob and I were spending our last evening together. Ma had finally agreed that he could spend the night with us in Campden Hill Square before travelling on, by an early train, to Bexhill.

We were alone, eating our supper in the kitchen. Ma and Tim had gone out to a party given by one of Tim's actor friends and, due to a misunderstanding, none of the staff would be back until the morning.

'I hate cold tongue.'

'Well, have some cold ham then.' I held out the plate.

He sighed, taking it from me. 'I suppose I must eat something. This is as putrid as supper at school. Surely

[175]

he could have done us better.' It was Tim who had gone out to a local delicatessen to buy us our food.

'He certainly would have done if he'd been buying for himself.'

'Smoked salmon,' Bob said.

'Caviare.'

'Pâté de foie gras.'

We both burst into laughter.

For a moment I had forgotten the car crash and Ma's illness on the train; or, if I had not forgotten them, I had pushed them out of my consciousness. I had also pushed out of my consciousness those increasingly frequent times when I had brooded on a world without Ma, either thinking: We could do It, we could do It!, or willing Bob to do It.

'I'm sorry you can't stay. I did try. But you know what Ma's like. Terribly obstinate.'

'Once a bitch, always a bitch. Well, it doesn't really matter. At least I'll see Jeanette.' This was the eleven-year-old girl at the summer school. 'Yes, I rather look forward to that.' He mused, smiling to himself. Then he looked up: 'But I'll miss you. In your own way, you're quite as good as Jeanette.'

'Oh, shut up!'

He laughed. 'Why do you have to be so embarrassed and ashamed? You don't think what we did was wrong, do you? Just a bit of fun. We're not queer, for God's sake. Variety is the spice of life – isn't that what they say?'

I munched on some ham. Then I leaned across the table to him. 'We'll still be friends at school, won't we?' I surprised myself with the question. Why shouldn't we be? What did I fear?

'I should think so. Why not? We're totally unlike

[176]

each other, in every possible way. But . . .' He raised his shoulders. 'The attraction of opposites.'

After dinner, we played jazz on the gramophone which had once belonged to Aunt Bertha. She had often played me Beethoven or Chopin or Schubert on it. I do not imagine that, while she was alive, a single jazz record had ever revolved on its turntable. The records which we were playing, of Joe Daniels and Harry Roy and Fred Elizalde, all belonged to Tim. Most of them Ma had given to him.

Suddenly, in the middle of a record of Nat Gonella, Bob jumped up and pulled off the needle, so violently that its squealing passage must have left a scratch. 'Oh, I can't go on listening to this bilge!' He threw himself back into the sofa. 'What are we going to do now? We could go out to a flick, I suppose. It's not too late.'

Suddenly, unbidden, an idea winged in to me. 'We could go upstairs.'

'Upstairs?'

'To Ma's room.'

He stared at me. I might have said something totally crazy.

'Or your room. Or my room.'

Then he began to laugh. He laughed more and more loudly, throwing back his head. 'Oh, no, no, no!'

'Why not? . . . Please. It'll be the last time for, oh, ages. Please!'

'Sorry. I'm just not in the mood.'

'Oh, come on!'

'Sorry. No can do.' He jumped up off the sofa. 'Let's go out to that flick.'

37

I awoke that morning, as I was so often to awake in the years ahead, with a feeling of terror. It was as though an invisible hand, almost throttling me, had shaken me out of sleep. Then I remembered: Bob would be leaving for Bexhill that morning. I put my head back on the pillow and stared at the opposite wall, criss-crossed with the first light through the thick lace curtains. always drew back the brown velvet curtains before switching off the light and getting into bed. I loved to wake to the glimmer of dawn and then, snuggling down into the bedclothes, to slip back into unconscious ness once again.

Bob would be leaving; and he did not have to leave It was Ma who was depriving me of him, just as it was Ma who had deprived me of Dad, intermittently ever since I was born and now permanently through her selfishness and callousness. *Delenda est*. That was what Bob had said and I had known enough Latin to under stand him. Between us, during the week ahead, before we went back to school, we might have indeed been able to destroy her. Bob, so much more intelligent and resourceful and so much more cool-headed than I would have thought of the perfect way. Then, once she had vanished, we would have had only each other and the money with which to do precisely what we wanted *Smoked salmon. Caviare. Pâté de foie gras*. That litany o ours over supper the previous evening now came back

me. I could hear Bob laughing, as we intoned each
delicacy.

Looking back now, I can only marvel at the extraordinary rage of my love for him at that moment. I was
never again to love any man in that fashion, let alone
with that same feverish intensity. Nor have I brought
that same feverish intensity to my love for Noreen. It
was a kind of madness; and yet a madness in which I
saw everything with total clarity and logic.

Neither Ma nor Tim came down that early to breakfast. The previous night, on her way up to bed, Ma had
said in an offhand way to Bob: 'Well, I'd better say
goodbye now. I won't be up in time to say goodbye
tomorrow.'

Bob had put out his hand, with its savagely bitten
nails (at that time even the thought of their ugliness
excited me) and reluctantly Ma had taken it. 'Thank
you so much, Mrs Frost. It was a really super time.'

'Yes, it was super, wasn't it?' Once again, merely by
repeating some word or phrase which Bob had said,
Ma had been able to mock him.

'Goodbye, Tim.'

'Goodbye, old chap. Have a good journey.'

Ma had put an arm round Tim's waist, and together
they had then begun to mount the wide staircase,
without a backward look.

Now Bob and I faced each other across the breakfast
table. From the chafing-dish on the sideboard, he had
helped himself liberally to sausage, bacon, grilled tomatoes, fried egg. I had taken merely a slice of toast.

He paused in shovelling his food into his mouth. 'Is
that all you're going to eat?'

'Somehow I don't feel hungry.'

'I'm eating for the whole week ahead. They never

[179]

give us anything but corn-flakes and bread and marga
ine for breakfast.'

Even with butter and marmalade, the toast fe
strangely dry and tasteless in my mouth. 'I wish yo
didn't have to go.'

He shrugged cheerfully. 'Well, that's how it is.'

'I hate her for not allowing you to stay. Why couldn
you stay? You wouldn't be in the way.'

'She must have had enough of me.' He grinnec
'After all, I'm not her One and Only.'

I had an absurd impulse to declare: 'No, but you'r
my One and Only.' Instead, I found myself saying: 'Yo
know, I miss my father so much. Last night I wa
thinking of him. And again this morning.'

It was true. I had so often groaned inwardly at th
thought of having to go to visit Dad; had so ofte
postponed doing so; had so often stayed with him fe
half an hour or even a mere quarter of an hour and ha
then hurried off. But now his absence was like
perpetual ache; and, as though in an effort to appeas
that ache, I was constantly dreaming of him, not
I had known him during those last unhappy montl
but as he had been when he had first come ba
from the Benedictine community and had seemed
be cured.

Bob put his head on one side, looking at me over h
raised fork. He shrugged. 'You'll get over it.'

*No, no, I shan't, I shan't! Any more than I'll get over yo
leaving me now.* But instead I merely said, with a sig
'Yes, I suppose I shall.'

For a while we sat in silence broken only by th
sound of toast crackling between his teeth or his slur
ing of his coffee. Then I asked, since I knew that a
return visit of his might depend on it: 'Did you lea
anything for Isabel?'

[180]

'Isabel?'

I pointed at the closed door between the dining-room
nd the kitchen. 'The maid.'

'What should I have left?'

'Well, a tip.' I put a hand into my trouser pocket and
ok out a half-crown. 'Leave that on the dressing-room
ble.'

He did not take the half-crown. 'Is that necessary?'

I nodded. 'Ma's sure to ask her.'

'But she's not *done* anything for me. I mean, she gets
aid anyway for making the bed and so on – doesn't
e?'

'Yes. But . . . well, it's expected.'

'I don't see why *you* should fork out the money – just
ecause I haven't got any to speak of.'

'Go on. Take it.'

Reluctantly, he took the coin from me. 'I never left
nything for Maria or Violetta,' he said.

'Yes, I know.'

'How do you know?'

'Ma told me.'

He threw back his head and laughed. 'She told you!
h, God, what an old cow! She must have asked them.'

'Yes, I suppose she must have.'

Then I too began to laugh.

nce again I carried the bag and he carried the battered,
rded suitcase, as we made our way down the hill to
e underground. He had been in such high spirits
ring breakfast, but now he was silent and glum.

In the Inner Circle train he said: 'Those were good
ys.'

'Yes, they were, weren't they?' Then I added: 'I think
e best of my life.'

He laughed. 'Isn't that something of a overstatement?'

'No. Not at all. Not at all.'

He looked at his watch and then raised it to his ea and shook it. 'This bloody thing has stopped again. need a new one. Perhaps your mother might conside giving me a Longines? Gold, of course.'

'If I had the money, I'd give you one.'

He looked at me, surprised, appraising. Then he sai in a slow, wondering voice: 'Yes, I believe you would.

At the entrance to the platform, I crossed over, penn in hand, to get a platform ticket from the machine. Bu he told me: 'No, don't get one of those! I hate bein seen off.'

'But I want to see you off.'

'No. I'd rather you didn't.'

I sighed. 'Okay.' I drew out my wallet. 'Bob – don be offended . . . don't refuse . . .'

He shook his head vehemently. 'No. *No!*'

I held out a pound note. 'It's not much. But I know you're dead broke. It'll help in the week ahead. Please

Briefly he hesitated. Then he took the note from m and stuffed it into the breast pocket of his Harris twee jacket. 'Thanks. You're a good pal.'

'We must spend another hols together.'

He grinned. 'Yes. We have so much unfinishe business.'

What did he mean? Did he mean what I hoped an thought that he meant?

'Well – so long!' He showed his ticket to the collecto and hefted first the suitcase, then the bag. He began t march off down the long platform, the trilby hat makin his head seem even bigger than usual.

I felt the tears pricking at my eyes. I felt my ange against Ma, frothily bilious, surging within me.

[182]

'Goodbye! Goodbye!' I called after him.
But he did not turn round.

38

'So our charity boy has gone.'

As I entered the hall, Ma came down the stairs in her new silk dressing-gown, bought in Milan, and feathered mules. She had beautiful feet, small, with high arches. Once, at the villa, I had seen, from my bedroom window, Tim holding one in his hands and kissing it, on the terrace below. I could understand his doing that.

'Do you mean Bob?' But of course I knew exactly whom she meant. Sometimes she would also refer to him as 'the remittance child'.

'Of course I mean Bob. Who else would I mean?'

'Yes, he's gone.'

'Oh, what a relief! I do hope that next time you decide to invite a school chum for the hols, you'll find someone a little more *sortable*.'

'Why do you keep using that word?'

'What word?'

'*Sortable*.'

'Well, I suppose I use it because there's no proper English equivalent. You *are* in a crosspatch mood.'

'Suitable. What's wrong with suitable?'

'What's wrong with it? Well, it's just not quite right. *Sortable* suggests a *social* unsuitability.'

She went into the dining-room and I followed her. As she raised the lid of the chafing-dish, I said: 'You've ruined this last week for me.'

'What do you mean? What *do* you mean?'

'By sending Bob away. He was my only company. You and Tim do everything together. I'm always alone.'

'Oh, nonsense! Stuff and nonsense!' She speared a rasher of bacon. 'Aren't we all going to the Royal Academy tomorrow?'

'Bob *could* have stayed. There was no reason why he couldn't have stayed.'

She turned on me, plate in hand. 'There were a number of reasons. I was tired of spending money on him. Tired of his gaucheness and – er – rudeness. Tired of his grubbiness. Tired of his total, absolutely total, lack of any kind of charm. You have the cheek to say that I've ruined this last week of your holidays. Well, that dreadful pal of yours ruined my whole holiday in Italy.'

Any further argument was interrupted by the ringing of the telephone. 'Oh, do answer it!' Ma snapped at me. 'God knows what those two women are doing!'

I went out into the hall and picked up the receiver. The operator quacked that it was a call from New York – a person-to-person call for Mr Timothy Packer.

'Who is it?' Ma was shouting from the dining-room. 'For God's sake, who is it?'

'It's for Tim. From America.'

'Well, call him then! Call him!'

Telling the operator to hold on, I raced up the stairs and banged on Tim's door. When, after a number of bangs, there was still no answer, I crossed over and banged on Ma's.

'Hello! Yes, yes!' Clearly I had woken him.

'Telephone! New York!'

'Oh, Christ! Coming, coming!'

His face flushed, his eyes bleary, his feet bare, in only his pyjama bottoms, he lurched through the door

[184]

What a bloody awful time to ring!' It was almost eleven.

Grumpily he picked up the receiver. Ma was now out in the hall, a cup of coffee in one hand. He scowled over at her, as he said: 'Yes, yes . . . This is Tim Packer here.' Then his face was irradiated. 'Oh, Aaron! *Aaron!* What a wonderful surprise.'

Ma drew in her breath sharply, then approached yet nearer to the telephone, in an effort to hear what was being said.

'. . . But that's terrific . . . Jane Austen's *Emma* . . . No, I can't say I've read it, you know what an ignoramus I am . . . Yes, of course, of course . . . Of *course* . . Would I like to do it? You must be joking!'

As the conversation prolonged itself, Ma kept saying: What is all this? What's this all about? What does he want?', until, placing a hand over the receiver, Tim told her brutally: 'For God's sake, shut up!'

Eventually, the conversation had ended. Reflectively, Tim put down the receiver. Then he looked up at us both and grinned. 'That was Aaron,' he announced, needlessly. 'There's a job in the offing. Jane Austen's *Emma*. Apparently there's a character in it – only a minor character, unfortunately, not one of the leads – and Aaron thinks that he might be just right for me. That Huxley man will be doing the script,' he added.

'Are they filming over here?'

'No. Oh, no. In Hollywood.' He burst into laughter. 'Perhaps at last, at long last, my luck is changing! I've always longed to go to Hollywood.' Then he sobered up. 'Of course it's by no means in the bag. The director may take against me. Who knows? All sorts of things could go wrong.'

Ma put down the cup of coffee on the hall table. Her already made-up mouth looked vividly red against the

pallor of her face. She was breathing heavily. 'You
mean – you have to go to America?'

"Fraid so, old darling. *Tout de suite* . . . Once I've had
a cup of coffee and a bath and got into some togs, I'l
have to rush round to Cook's to see about a passage.'

'But you're not going to leave me?' Ma was
incredulous.

'I'm not going to leave you *for ever*, sweetie. Just for a
week or two – or a month or two, *if* I get the job.'

'But this is terrible!' Ma sank down on to a chair
'This is absolutely terrible! How can I manage withou
you? You're The One and Only. Without you, I'll be' –
her face began to crumple – 'I'll be totally lost. Oh, Tim
Tim, how can you be so cruel? How can you?'

'Now, come on, darling.' Tim put an arm round he
shoulder. Then he knelt beside her. 'It's not all tha
bad.' He laughed. 'Wouldn't you like me to becom
another Ronald Colman?'

Ma raised the hem of her silk dressing-gown and
wiped her eyes on it. 'Of course I want you to succeed
. . . want you to become famous . . .' She looked
imploringly at him. 'Perhaps I could accompany you
Wouldn't that be possible?'

Tim's face set into hard lines of exasperation. 'No
I'm afraid it would not. Emphatically it would not. Thi
is a business trip. If you came, I'd be able to spend ver
little time with you. Frankly, you'd be in the way!'

'In the way!' Ma wailed it. 'What a cruel thing to te
me!'

At that point, I decided that I could take no more
Mess, mess, mess! Why did she have to make such
horrendous mess of everything? I was sickened by thi
public vomiting out of the emotions on which sh
constantly gorged herself.

From the sitting-room, where I sat with Ma's *Dail*

[186]

Sketch, I tried not to listen to them continuing to shout at each other. But it was impossible not to do so. At one moment Tim yelled at Ma: 'You stupid old cunt!' and at another moment I heard her sobbing – 'Cruel, cruel, cruel.' Then their voices became less and less furious, less and less audible. 'Oh, never mind, never mind!' I caught Ma crooning.

Not long after that, I heard them going up the stairs. I knew where they were going. I knew what they were planning to do.

I put down the copy of the *Daily Sketch*. I felt at once nauseated and excited. I thought of Ma's bed, with its pink sheets and pink eiderdown and damask silk cover of a darker pink. I thought of those mountainous, down-filled pillows of hers and the light filtering through the thick curtains. I thought of her and Tim lying pressed to each other, limbs inextricably entangled, as once, so many years before, I had seen Ma and Fergus lying pressed to each other, limbs inextricably entangled, in their Ritz Hotel bedroom in Barcelona.

Then suddenly Bob became Tim and I became Ma, and it was he and I on the bed, with Ma's scent, that scent which even now I associate with her, lemony, sharp, almost peppery, filling my nostrils.

39

Tim had said that his luggage looked awfully shabby for Hollywood – 'people judge one so much by appearances over there' – and so Ma had bought him the two crocodile-leather suitcases which now stood in the hall.

Ma had wanted to accompany him to Southampton, where he would be boarding the *Queen Mary*, but he had said no to that. He had also said no, precipitating yet another row, when she had said that then at least she would see him off at Waterloo. 'I know why you don't want me to come,' she had told him. 'You're meeting that dreadful queen.'

'Aaron is in the States,' Tim had told her with icy disdain. 'So how on earth can he be my travelling companion?'

'Well, then you're meeting someone else.'

'I am meeting nobody, nobody at all. Just get that into your head. I just hate being seen off. I always have hated it.'

Now, all this previous acrimony forgotten, they kept reminding each other to write, to telephone, to take care of themselves, not to do anything silly, not to forget each other.

'What's happened to that bloody taxi?' Yet again Tim looked at the Longines watch. 'I don't want to miss that boat-train.'

'You're not going to miss it. There's oceans of time.'

'Suppose we get held up in a traffic jam?' Tim was clearly one of those people who suffer from *Reiseangst*. 'Suppose the taxi breaks down?'

'Oh, darling, I'm going to miss you. I'm going to miss you so, so much.' Tears now running down her cheeks, Ma threw her arms around him.

Perfunctorily Tim patted her back. 'And I'm going to miss you, sweetie.'

'You know that you're my One and Only. There's never been anyone like you. There never *can* be anyone like you.' Then she abruptly let go of him. 'Oh, God, I'd almost forgotten!'

'What is it?'

She began to race up the stairs. As soon as she had disappeared, there was a ring at the door. Tim rushed over and pulled it open. It was the taxi-driver, a muffler wound round and round his scrawny neck, its end trailing down his back, despite the summer heat.

'Bella!' Tim yelled. *'Bella!* The taxi's come. Oh, what the hell is she doing?' He turned to the driver. 'Those are the two bags,' he said.

Ma came clattering down the stairs. 'I wanted you to take this. As a keepsake. A good-luck talisman.' She gave a high, hysterical laugh. 'My marker. To say – this property belongs to me – so, hands off.'

She was holding out something to him, saying: 'Put it on, put it on! I hope to God it fits.'

What was it? I went forward, peered.

Tim placed the ring on his little finger. Then he held out his hand to us: 'Perfect. Absolutely perfect.'

The ring was Dad's signet ring.

40

'Do you really think you'll be all right on your own?'

'Yes, of course.'

'I don't have to go today.'

'Yes, you do. The sooner you go, the better. You know that. It's been preying on your mind.' Noreen sighs, as she holds up two dried leaves to the light and squints at them, wondering which of them to use for her collage. 'Not that you're likely to get anywhere,' she says, voicing my own pessimism. 'He's not the sort of person to listen to an appeal.'

Yesterday evening she had what she called 'a nasty turn'. I heard a bang from the kitchen, followed by a groan, and rushed in from the sitting-room, still clutching the cutlery which I had been about to place on the table for our supper. Her copy of Elizabeth David's *Mediterranean Food* lay, open face downwards, on the tiles by the stove, with her glasses, fortunately unbroken, lying beside it. How had she lost the glasses? We neither of us could imagine. She herself was propped sideways on the kitchen chair closest to the stove, on her face an expression of dismay and bewilderment.

'What happened? Are you all right?'

'I don't know.' There was an oddness in the way in which she seemed to be forcing the reluctant words, one after the other, out of her half-closed lips. 'Suddenly . . . I don't know . . . I had no idea where I was or who I was or what I was doing . . .'

I went over to her and put my arms about her. 'Anyway, you're all right now. Thank God.'

'Yes, I'm all right now,' she replied in a low, perplexed voice. 'I'd better get back to preparing the supper.'

'Certainly not. I'll see to it.'

'But you're tired. You did all that gardening.'

'I'm not in the least tired,' I answered, untruthfully. 'Now you go and put your legs up on the sofa. Come on! I'll help you.'

Now she says: 'I was thinking last night . . . If he says no – if he won't make any changes . . . It needn't be the end of the world.'

I say nothing. What can I say? Of course it will be the end of the world, of our world, of this cosy little world of respectability and habit and mutual love, which, oh so laboriously, we have constructed for ourselves over the last forty and more years. How, for a start, are we

[190]

ever going to sell the shop and the house, at a period when no one can sell anything? And how, at our ages, are we going to acquire new customers and new friends under some other name in some other village, remote from this one, or even in some other country?

'We've got each other,' she goes on. But the consolatory cliché has no power to console me. I doubt if it even consoles her.

I kiss her goodbye, first on the cheek, then on the forehead and then on the mouth. I have never kissed her three times over like that before. It is almost as though I were saying goodbye to her for ever. 'Now take care of yourself. Don't overdo things.'

She gazes up at me, holding my hand in her own twisted, knobbly one. 'Good luck,' she says. Appalled, profoundly moved, I see that there are tears in her eyes.

As, brief-case weighed down with Bob's manuscript in one hand, I emerge into the street, I spot Ivor outside the greengrocer's opposite. He is in conversation with an elderly couple whom I often see but whom I do not know. Pray God I can get into the car unnoticed! But, abruptly excusing himself, he is racing across the road, in the path of an oncoming lorry. I can see the face of the lorry-driver contorted in rage; he hoots and hoots again.

'Maurice! Maurice!'

I have to halt before our garage, which is next door to the house.

'You've heard the news, haven't you?'

'What news?'

'They've gone! Done a bunk! Can you believe it? Up sticks and gone!'

For a moment I have no idea of whom he is talking. Then I realise that it must be of Jack and Iris.

'What a scandal! Everyone in the village is talking of nothing else this morning. I'm amazed you haven't heard already.'

He goes on like this for a while. Then I say: 'I'm terribly sorry, Ivor. I must get going. An appointment.'

'Yes, of course, of course, old boy. But what a scandal, what a scandal! In all the years I've lived here, we've never had such a scandal.'

41

Ma stood in the doorway as the taxi moved off down the hill. One hand was raised in a last, forlorn farewell, but Tim did not look back. When the taxi had swivelled into Holland Park Avenue and vanished from sight, she turned away, hand to forehead, and then let out an inarticulate wail. This was followed by an 'Oh, God! God, God, God!' Without even glancing at me, her face contorted, she raced into the drawing-room, threw herself on to a sofa, and began to sob, so violently that it sounded as though she were retching against the cushion pressed to her cheek.

The room, shadowy and smelling of cigarette smoke and booze, was in the condition in which she and Tim had left it in the early hours. No doubt soon Isabel would come in, to jerk back the curtains, to take away the brimming ashtrays, the dirty glasses and the empty bottles, and to straighten and pat the cushions. As I walked across the carpet, rage made me feel so giddy that I staggered as though on a high sea.

I stood over her. 'Why did you do that?'

Continuing to sob, she made no answer. She might never have heard me.

'Why did you do that? Why did you give him Dad's signet ring? It has the crest of the family on it. That should have been mine.'

Now she twisted her face, red and tear-stained, up and round in order to stare at me. She looked astonished. 'What are you talking about?' she asked me. 'What *are* you talking about?'

'Dad's ring. Dad's signet ring.' Still she did not answer. 'Can't you hear what I'm saying?' I leaned over and grabbed her arm. I jerked her up into a sitting position.

'Ouch! You're hurting me. Don't do that!' Then she said: 'I gave it to him because I wanted to give it to him. I was your father's only legatee. Everything that belonged to him came to me. You know that perfectly well.' Then she was crying again. 'Why, why, why do you have to start all this now? Can't you see how upset I am? Oh, do leave me alone!'

'I'm also upset,' I said.

'You! You're too cold a fish to be upset, really upset about anything at all. There's not a hope in hell of making you understand what Tim's going like this means to me. Not a hope! Once he's over there – out of my sight – anything, anything at all could happen. I may never see him again! I just can't live without him. He's The One and Only. I know there've been others but he's . . .'

'Oh, stop using that silly One and Only! Stop it! You're only interested in him because he fucks you. That's all. He's a good fuck, the best you've ever had. That's it, isn't it? Isn't it?' Once again I grabbed her arm. I began to shake it.

'Stop that! Stop!' Suddenly she looked terrified.

[193]

'Why did you give him Dad's signet ring?' I repeated.

'Because I wanted him to have something to remember me by.'

'But you've given him so much else. Much more valuable things. The cigarette lighter. That Fabergé cigarette case. The watch. All those clothes. The car. That ring was *mine*! It belonged in the family.'

'Tim *is* family. He's one of us now. Anyway I can always have another, similar ring engraved for you. We can to go Mappin & Webb today. Any day. Whenever you like. But schoolboys don't wear rings.'

'It was *mine*, you bitch! It was mine because it was Dad's.'

By now I had released her. Rubbing her bruised arm, she put her head on one side, tongue between lips, and then burst into laughter. 'All this Dad, Dad, Dad! You don't know – nobody knows – if he was really your Dad.' She hesitated for a moment. Then she said: 'My guess is, he wasn't.'

'What the hell are you talking about?' Once again, as on the train, I was experiencing that weird hallucination. Everything at which I looked – the soiled glasses, the overflowing ashtrays, the cushions on the sofa, Ma's blotched, derisive face – seemed to be pulsating in and out, in and out, in time to the ever more insistent thudding of my heart.

'Unlike Tim, he was never any good at it. And at the time . . . well, there were . . .'

Beside the sofa, on the low table, there were two empty cocktail glasses and the chrome-plated cocktail shaker, a plate with a partially shaved lemon on it, and the knife, small but sharp, which Tim always used to do the shaving. I grabbed the knife, and almost at the same moment she screamed and then, even more piercing, screamed a second time. In a frenzy (that was how it was repeatedly described in court), I stabbed her over and over again. Forty-seven times was the count. Curiously the only thing that I could later remember of the stabbing was blood of hers splashing up on to my lips and of my tasting it, metallic and bitter.

Isabel heard the screams. She appeared for an instant in the doorway of the drawing-room (of course I did not notice her) and then, yelping in terror, she rushed out of the house. In the distance she saw the horse-drawn cart of the milkman, so soon to be killed at Dunkirk. The milkman rang the bell of the Braceys' house and hammered on the door.

When the police arrived, I was sitting on a straight-backed chair by the window.

They tried to question me but I said nothing. I continued to say nothing until, three years later, Noreen made me say that first Yes and so, eventually, retrieved me from the Black Box.

42

It is now not so much a village as a suburb of Canterbury. I enter an area of what seems to be waste land, dotted with an occasional tree, and then pass through a housing estate, high, symmetrical blocks of flats ranged in rectangles around concrete areas which are littered, even at this hour of the morning, with surprisingly expensive-looking cars. Beyond the housing estate rises a small wooded hill, towards which, having yet again consulted the map, I begin to make my way. I pass one drive, leading up to an invisible house, and then another drive, this one leading up to a squat bungalow set back from a scrupulously kept garden, with a red setter asleep on the lawn.

Then I see the gate, with 'Meadowlands' inscribed on it. Where are the meadowlands? Presumably once, before the high-rise blocks were erected, there were green fields around the hill, and cows and horses browsed there.

The house is a large red-brick Victorian one, with two high, narrow gables and a porch from which the olive-green paint is flaking. At some recent date an ugly concrete garage was attached to one side. Its doors open, it is empty. Can this mean that Bob is away or out? Noreen repeatedly urged me to telephone him first. That I did not do so was because I feared that he might then refuse to see me.

The kidney-shaped patch of lawn needs cutting, the laurels around the house need pruning, and clumps of weeds are obdurately thrusting up through the gravel of the drive. A child's gym shoe lies discarded in a flower-bed full of straggling roses, and a plastic bag dangles from a high branch of the chestnut tree which soars up over the garage.

Slowly, fearfully I get out of the car and shut the door. Then I remember the brief-case with the type-script in it, and I open the door again. After that, I ring at the bell, wait, ring again. My heart has set up an uncomfortable drumming within me, which seems also to administer jolt after jolt to my brain.

'Yes?' The door has opened; the voice is irritable.

'Bob.'

He peers up at me, clearly not recognising me. I might not have recognised him, but for that head which, above a sadly shrunken, stooped body, now seems even more disproportionate than before. Then a vague suspicion flickers in his eyes. 'You're . . . Good God! It's Mervyn!'

I smile. 'Not Mervyn now. Not even Otto Cramp. Maurice. Remember?'

'Maurice! Yes, of course, of course! Come in, dear chap, come in! Forgive the mess – all this mess.' He gestures around him, having backed into the hall. Two children's bicycles are propped against a wall. A child's T-shirt lies on the floor, beside a gym shoe which presumably makes up a pair with the one in the flower-bed. *The Times* and the *Guardian* are still on the door-mat.

'Laura is away with the kids in our cottage in Wales. I thought it a good opportunity to put the finishing touches to the book.'

'You mean the autobiography?'

He nods; then extends a hand. The nails, I notice, are still savagely bitten to the quick. 'Let me take that from you.' Reluctantly I hand over the brief-case and he then places it on the hall table. He grins at me. 'Well, what a surprise! I hardly recognised you after all these years.'

'I hardly recognised you.' His eyes look huge behind his thick, horn-rimmed glasses; his forehead is corru-gated, and there is a network of red and purple veins over his cheeks and nose. I realise that he has not shaved this morning.

'Time isn't kind. Is it?'

He leads me into a long, high-ceilinged sitting-room, as untidy as the hall. There are a few good pieces of furniture in it and, surprisingly, some even better pictures – I at once recognise a Burra and a Piper and guess that the one beyond them must be a Bomberg. As I cross over to examine the possible Bomberg – yes, I was right, there in a corner is the signature – Bob says: 'It's a shame Laura's missed you. She shares your

[197]

interests. As you know, I never had any visual sense at all. Just as you never had any scientific sense.'

I know from the autobiography that Laura is his second wife and that he has two young children, a girl and a boy, by her, in addition to the two grown-up daughters by his previous, French wife, now dead.

'I feel that I now know far more about you than you know about me,' I say. Puzzled, his now shaggy white eyebrows almost joined, he stares at me. 'I mean – after reading your book,' I explain.

He laughs. 'Yes, it is rather a give-away!' He removes some knitting from an armchair and points at it. 'Sit down! Sit down!'

I sit. The seat, springs broken, subsides uncomfortably under my weight. He perches on the arm of the chair opposite to me, head cocked to one side and those hands, with their stubby fingers and cruelly bitten nails, interlocked. He smiles. 'You were passing, I suppose?'

'No. I came because I had to come.'

'Oh!' He grins. 'You mean you made a special journey? That sounds terribly serious.'

'It *is* serious. For me.'

Now he slides sideways into the chair, on the arm of which he has so far been perching. He raises his left hand to his mouth and begins to gnaw at the nail of the little finger. I want to say: 'Oh, do stop doing that!', as I used to do at Gladbury. The habit always nauseated me.

'Tell me,' he says.

I sigh. 'Why did you send me that typescript?' I get up, go out to the hall, and fetch my brief-case. I open it. 'This.' I pull out the typescript and hold it out to him. He takes it from me, looks at one page and then another, as though it were something that he has never seen before, and then places it on his lap.

[198]

'I thought it would interest you. Since there's so much about you in it.' He leans forward. 'Didn't it interest you? I'm rather pleased with it. I – I think it could have a modest success. Laura thinks so too, and she was in publishing before we met.'

'Anyone – any journalist – who reads that book will know exactly how to find me. Why on earth do you have to be so *specific*?'

He jumps up from the chair. 'Let's go and have some grub. I was just about to get my lunch. Cold, I'm afraid. I never could cook. Laura's terrific. Like you – if I remember correctly.'

'I don't feel at all hungry.'

'Oh, come on. *L'appétit vient en mangeant*. You know that.'

Angry at the interruption, I follow him down the hall to the large kitchen at the end. Its window overlooks a shabby back garden, with two corrugated iron sheds at the bottom of it. Used crockery and glasses are piled everywhere. He pushes some plates to one side on the kitchen table and then, having tugged out its warped drawer, removes some bone-handled knives and forks. 'Let's see what we have.' He opens the refrigerator and stoops to peer into it. 'There's some cold ham here and some coleslaw. Oh, and I think there are some tomatoes. How does that strike you?'

'I don't feel at all hungry,' I repeat. 'Anything will do.'

Now from a rack by the old-fashioned sink he is getting down some plates. They are Belleek, I realise at once from their mother-of-pearl lustre; but one of them is cracked and the other, with a dark, diagonal fissure across it, must have been clumsily repaired. As he continues with the preparations, I stand leaning against the sink. I am in a fury of impatience.

'Yes, yes, this *is* a surprise. But a most welcome one. *Most* welcome. When did we last see each other? It must be years and years ago. Of course we wrote for a while. That's how I knew that you had set yourself up – or, rather, Noreen had set you up – in that little shop of yours. Once Laura and I were driving past it and we all but called in. But we were already late for lunch with some friends in Brighton . . .'

I hardly hear him as he goes on and on.

Now at last we are facing each other across the table. 'I hope this ham is okay. It's almost a week old. But it's been in the fridge all the time. What do you think?'

'I'm sure it's all right.' I spear a single piece with my fork from the pile on the grease-proof paper which he is holding out to me.

'Is that sufficient for you?'

Suddenly it comes back to me – God knows why – that Ma often used to tell me that it was 'vulgar' or 'common' to say 'sufficient' instead of 'enough'.

'Yes. Fine. Thank you.'

He picks up the old-fashioned knife, blotched with rust, and holds it over a loaf of granary bread. 'A slice of bread?'

I shake my head.

Then I lean forward: 'There's another thing – if you had to be so specific about everything else, why did I have to become Otto Cramp?'

He throws himself back in his chair, with such violence that it is amazing that it does not tip over. He laughs uproariously. 'Otto Cramp! I rather liked that name. It seemed – somehow – to express all the essential things that you are.'

'What do you mean?'

'Well, something Germanic. That's the Otto part. And then . . . there's always been something *clenched*

[200]

about you. Something tightly closed, something under – under enormous tension. No?' He pops some ham into his mouth. 'Hence the Cramp. Tension creates cramp. As in a fist which one keeps tightly closed for far too long.' He chews. 'I'm sorry you don't like it.'

'What I'm trying to get at is . . . It's so inconsistent to change our names and yet not to change the name of the village and – and all the other details about us . . .'

He shrugs. 'Would you like me to give your real names?'

'No. Of course not. No!'

'An autobiography *has* to be specific. It's not a novel. You can't tamper with the facts – any more than you can tamper with the facts if you're a scientist. I had to put down the facts.'

'Why did you have to write of – of all that?' By 'all that' I mean, of course, It and the Black Box.

'Well . . .' He leans back in his chair, thinking for a moment. 'It was an important part of my life. Wasn't it? You and your mother and Tim and Como were all an important part of my life. Sometimes – sometimes I think – the most important part. You can't write an account of your life and then leave out the most important part. Can you? Anyway, your story was also a part of my thesis – the whole thesis of my book.'

I shake my head. 'I don't understand.'

He laughs. 'I suspect that you've read only what I've written about *you*.'

'No. I've read the whole book.'

'Well, then . . . As you know, I call it *Blue Genes*. Laura thinks that a thoroughly silly title and I have a feeling she is right. No doubt I'll think of something better. But the point is that the one thread running through the book is my life's work – my life's obsession if you prefer it. Genetics. Ordinary people are frightened of genetics. And geneticists are frightened that ordinary people are frightened. Because the fear of ordinary people can so easily turn into loathing.'

'I don't understand.'

'That doesn't surprise me. You were always dim about anything scientific. Why are ordinary people frightened of people like me? Because we geneticists tell them that their genes – and not their upbringing or their environment – have made them what they are. Because we geneticists deny them the comforting belief that all men are created equal. Intelligence, like almost everything else about us, is hereditable. One day someone – not perhaps in our lifetimes – will be able to take a single embryo cell and predict the exact degree of intelligence of the child eventually born from it.' He stuffs some more ham into his mouth. 'Have you got me so far?'

I nod.

'These are things which few geneticists dare to say except among themselves. Intelligence is inherited, homosexuality is inherited, a propensity to crime is inherited. We are all moving in predestined grooves – trams, not buses! But that's a truth which even geneticists refuse to face. Have you heard of Professor Kline, Professor Paul Kline of Exeter University? No, of course you haven't! Well, in a recent book of his, with the title *Intelligence: The Psychometric View*, he recommends, actually recommends, that scientists should sacrifice the interests of objective truth to what he calls "the humaneness of the person"! I ask you!' Suddenly vehement, he leans across to me. 'If a scientist doesn't live for the objective truth, then he should not be living at all. What a fool!'

'The humaneness of the person must be important too.'

[202]

'Not as important as the truth. Not for me at least. I once gave a lecture in New York in which I pointed out that, in objective, totally objective, intelligence tests, black Americans score some twenty per cent less than white ones. You can imagine the stink! Abusive letters. Threats to kill me even. A boycott by my students. That's why I'm now back here, instead of being over there. There are certain truths which are now, literally, unspeakable.'

He stares across at me, and with difficulty I stare back. Then I ask: 'What has all this got to do with me?'

'Well . . . Your case has always interested me. It struck me from the beginning – when you went, well, berserk and did something so horrendous, so unbeliev-able, so totally out of keeping with your character as everyone had known it – that this was a case not of nurture but of nature being responsible . . .' He holds out the packet of ham and, when I shake my head impatiently, says: 'No? Are you sure?' Then he goes on: 'Your family has a long history of irrationality and violence. Hasn't it? On both sides. Your mother had those rages, when she would suddenly begin hurling plates and vases and anything else to hand. Her grand-father was that general who ordered the Bhopal massa-cre and was never subsequently prepared to admit he had done anything reprehensible in causing the deaths of – what? – three hundred or so largely innocent people. Your mother's cousin went to prison for that vicious assault – not the first – on a policeman when he was drunk. Then there was your father. Suicide – almost everyone now agrees – is an act of aggression. Short of killing someone else, there is no more aggress-ive action. Your father might have killed your mother. Instead, he killed himself. I find all this fascinating. So,

[203]

you see, I felt that your story – and the story of your family – was highly relevant to the thesis of my book.'

I stare at him with, yes, a literally murderous hatred. Then I say: 'But you know – you must know – that if it hadn't been for you, I'd never have . . .'

'Oh, come on! Come *on!*' He bursts into laughter. 'What on earth do you mean?'

'It was you who put the idea into my head. You – you – *inspired* me to do it.'

'*I?*' He raises his hand to his chest and taps on it with a forefinger. '*I?* What the hell do you mean?'

'You know what I mean. You yourself made those two tries.'

He shakes his head. 'Sorry. I'm not following you.'

'The accident to the car. Ma's illness on the train.'

'You don't think . . .?' His incredulity seems to be wholly genuine. 'I had nothing, nothing whatever, to do with either of those things . . . Yes, I know we *talked* of bumping her off. But that was a joke. A joke between silly schoolboys. For God's sake, that was a joke!'

'It wasn't a joke to me.'

'You mean you seriously thought . . .?'

I do not answer.

'Incredible!'

'In a strange way – when I killed her . . .' I am going to say: I killed her for you. But I shake my head, waving a hand in front of it, as though some fly were annoying me with its buzzing.

'If I'd *inspired* you – as you put it – surely you'd have been a little more careful of the method you chose? No? When we used to joke like that about bumping her off, we were always thinking of foolproof methods. Remember? *Foolproof.* Insulin. Oxalic acid. A faked fall. Your method was hardly foolproof.' He laughs. 'You couldn't have made more sure that you were caught

[204]

red-handed. Literally,' he adds with a grin. 'And that was the saving of you. If it had all been premeditated – well, things would have been far less easy for you. Who would then have believed that you'd lost your marbles?'

I close my eyes. I am dazed. I don't know what to think. If it hadn't been for him, then I'd never have killed Ma: that is all I know.

I push back my chair. I have a sudden feeling that I am going to vomit. Then I say: 'Bob . . . you were once my closest friend. Do something for me. Please. *Please!*'

'What do you want me to do?' He pours some more wine into my glass. 'Well?'

'Cut all that out. All that about me. It's not necessary. It's not essential.'

Slowly he shakes his head, smiling as he does so. 'Sorry. No can do. I've explained to you. It's – it's an integral part of the book.'

'Not for me. Not just for me. For Noreen.'

'Why should I do anything for Noreen?' His dismissiveness is brutal. 'I hardly know her. She hates my guts.'

'Because she's ill, very ill. A lot of publicity would kill her.'

Again he shakes his head, with that same rueful smile. 'No can do.'

Without realising it, I put my hand out to the rusty bread-knife and pick it up.

He looks down at the knife. He is not in the least alarmed. 'Are you planning to stab me too?'

Was I? Yes, for a moment I was. I put down the knife.

'Please,' I say. 'For the sake of our friendship.'

He considers. Then he says: 'For the sake of our friendship?' He pushes back his chair, perfunctorily wipes his mouth on his paper napkin, gets to his feet.

[205]

'All right. I'll make a bargain with you. I'll do what you ask for the sake of our friendship if, in return – for the sake of our friendship – you'll do something for me.'

I stare at him in bewilderment and a kind of premonitory dread. 'What?' I say. 'What do you want?'

'Come.' He beckons to me. *'Come!'*

I get to my feet and follow him, still with that bewilderment and premonitory dread, out of the kitchen and down the corridor and up the wide stairs. We go into a large, damp bedroom, with clothes and newspapers and dirty cups and glasses scattered here and there. There is a large brass bed, with its sheet and single blanket twisted and grey. Some pyjamas have been tossed across it.

He says: 'Undress.'

I stare at him in amazement.

Quietly he repeats: 'Undress.'

I have hoped all along and feared all along and known all along that one day this will happen. With a sigh, I begin to take off my clothes, slowly, as though it were some ritual, long forgotten and now being resuscitated.

He is taking off his clothes. Ma always used to remark on the grubbiness of his underclothes. They are grubby now.

He puts his arms around me and then we tumble on to the soiled, unmade bed, in which no doubt he and his Laura always sleep together.

But now, as his arms tighten around me and I feel his mouth on mine, the bed is not theirs but Ma's, with its pink sheets and pillows and its darker pink damask silk bed-cover; and that potent smell is not a smell of wine, cigarettes and stale sweat but hers, uniquely, intoxicatingly hers, lemony, sharp, slightly peppery; and we ourselves are not two elderly men but two young boys, greedy, ardent, exhilarated, each The One and Only for the other . . .

'Give me the typescript.'

I go to the chair where he has left it and hand it to him. He walks down the corridor to the kitchen and I follow after. He pulls open the ancient Esso stove and chucks in the thick wad of paper. But it refuses to ignite. 'Oh, God!' he exclaims. 'I think I've let it go out. Laura will be furious with me. She's coming back this evening. I'll leave the damper open. Let's see what happens.' He raises a hand to his forehead, rubs it. 'Do you remember . . . in Bellagio . . . those roses I gave your mother . . . in the incinerator . . .?' Then he laughs: 'Anyway' – he points to the typescript on top of the clinkers – 'this was only a symbolic gesture. I have other copies.' He stoops and peers up into my face. He knows what I am thinking and he is only amused, not hurt or annoyed. 'No. Don't worry. I'm not planning to break my word. A bargain is a bargain, after all. I'm going to remove all trace of you.'

I wish that I could remove all trace of him. But now I know that I never can.

43

On the journey home, I keep repeating to myself, as though I were repeating it to Noreen: 'I did it to save you. I had to do it. Otherwise the book would have killed you.'

But I know that that is not why I did it. When he said goodbye to me, by the front door, he suddenly once again put both arms around me, and pressed his lips to mine. Then, with a laugh, he released me: 'Thoughts have power. Dreams have power. Wishes have power,' he whispered. Then he added: 'Time regained.'

Yes, on that rumpled, grimy bed, time was regained for me. From one Black Box I had passed, without knowing it, into another, larger Black Box, with Noreen as my fellow prisoner – or do I mean my gaoler? Now, giddily disorientated, I am free of both Black Boxes and am out in the open.

I leave the car not in the garage but out in the street, hoping that no traffic warden will see it. Then I open the front door and call: 'Noreen! *Noreen!*'

No answer comes.

'*Noreen!*'

Then I race up the stairs.

She is lying diagonally across the bed, with her knees drawn up and a hand under one cheek. At first I think that she is only asleep. Then I see the patch of dried blood on the pillow, just below her mouth.

As I move slowly towards her, with a mingling of horror and dread, I tread on something.

It is the glitterwax rose, which I made for her so many years ago. It must have fallen from her hand at the moment when she died.

Or, at least, that is what I want to think and try to think.